BRIDES OF BLESSINGS

Love More Precious Than Gold

BLESSED BEYOND
MEASURE

KARI TRUMBO

Blessed Beyond Measure

Cover Design by Carpe Librum Book Design
Edited by Hart's Reader Pulse

For anyone certain that they are unworthy of love, there is nothing that can separate you from the love that is in Christ Jesus. Nothing.

CHAPTER 1

The Steamboat Sophie,
Winter 1850

Lenora clutched her shawl about her shoulders at the rail of the ship as the wind whipped her skirts about her ankles. Cold sea air drove spray into her face, but she no longer felt it. Her little room was too cramped to stay inside. And there was the scenery above ... not just the endless ocean, but the man who'd started invading her every waking thought.

The waves rocked the steamer, but her stomach had long-since tired of trying to feel at-ease. If anything, the longer she was aboard ship, the more she detested it and would never offer to board again, not that it mattered. They were on their way to California, land of a million dreams, and there she would remain. Blessings ... she'd clutched to the name like a life raft since they'd left so long ago.

She'd heard rumors while standing at that very spot by the rail, rumors of landfall at the Isthmus of Panama. After six months at sea, solid land beneath her feet would be a blessed treat. It didn't matter that she'd also heard of rats the size of small dogs, bugs that could kill her, and monkeys that screamed loud enough to be heard miles away. It was land, and solid ground would mean her stomach could stop pitching.

Seven months before, in the early spring, her father had received a message from an old associate in need of help in California. Mr. Winslet had requested they come *post haste* to help him in building a land office in the new town of Blessings. He had miners that came and went aplenty, but he was looking to make Blessings into more than just a mining town. Mr. Winslet had a dream of building a place where people would be happy, share life, and grow old with him. Her father had made the decision, almost overnight, that they would all go. After a month of selling everything they wouldn't need and hiring two men to come with them as protection, they'd left everything she knew behind.

In a new town, Lenora could finally escape the expectation that she would be little more than a pretty face for a future husband to dote over and pat on the head. Her father had tried to rein in her pesky desires to become a lawyer like himself, but that had only made her crave it more. She could stretch herself, do something with the talents the Lord had given her. Be something in a little town that would expect every member to pull their weight to make it a success. After so many months at sea, she would never offer to return; Boston never held her heart, but the little town she'd never seen, did.

Mr. Abernathy was late. She'd have to go back below soon, or her mother would turn furious. A quick glance behind her, and she turned back to the vast ocean to hide her smile. Victor Abernathy approached with his usual swagger. Her skin prickled to life, just as it would if the sun had landed upon her. Anticipation of verbally sparring with him heated her up more than her thin shawl ever could. He was a man well used to anyone's bed but his own, or so he claimed, and he'd been pestering her almost from the start. Whenever her father wasn't around to take notice, he would appear.

Though she'd always been told she was beautiful, she'd never attracted the attention of a man with such an air of danger about him. His dark caramel hair had grown long on the ship, but he didn't seem to mind, using it instead to appear even more devilishly handsome as it whipped around his face in the blustery gale. He leaned against the rail next to her, confidence the very fiber of his clothing. His eyes, greener than the sea, ablaze just for her, took her in with an appreciative nod. No, this man wasn't for her. But keeping him away was a wonderful daily challenge that drove her to seek the open space of the deck whenever the weather would permit, and even like today, when it was questionable.

"Miss Farnsworth, pleasant day." He tipped his bowler hat and let his jade eyes wander liberally over her face, almost like a true caress.

"Some might claim it. It seemed rather cool to me." The rumor of land had said that it would get warmer as they approached landfall, but without that hope, the sea still left her cold to the bone.

She pulled the shawl tighter. There was nothing decent about Victor Abernathy, and if she knew what was good for her, she'd stay away. So, why did she always find herself at the rail, looking over her shoulder to see if he would draw near, hoping he would notice her standing there? He was so very different from all the men her father had introduced her to, hoping to build business relations between families. Abernathy was exciting, and completely forbidden. He stood too close to her, spoke flippantly, and didn't hide his tendencies nor his desires, like so many other men did.

Her father had hired him and another man, Cort, to accompany them to California. The other man stayed mostly hidden, watching them from a distance. She forgot about him most of the time. But not Abernathy. He was far from subtle. Every day, just when she was sure he wasn't going to come pester her that day, he would appear. And before they finished speaking, he'd have her heart beating erratically with his witty banter. No man from Boston had ever done that.

"Come now, my lovely, is my company so poor that you can't even have a smile when I'm about? Even a little one? Have a care, and tip those lovely lips just for me."

He moved to lean his hip against the railing and she fought the urge to push him off into the churning waters. Then his pestering would stop. But she wouldn't, because, despite what she made him think, no one had ever challenged her like Mr. Abernathy. Nor could anyone make her feel alive as he did. There was little doubt that he'd also *offered his time* to other women on the ship, which had made his pursuit of her less special, but he *was* a cad. Either she could allow herself to enjoy the mental stimulation of his visits, or let her mind wander to how many skirts he'd chased and let it get to her. She'd chosen to ignore his ignoble pastimes and enjoy the stolen moments he spent with her, chaste though they were.

"My father hired you to watch over my family. My *entire* family, Mr. Abernathy. I would think you would be a little more serious."

He sighed, and his firm lips parted just a bit, his eyes twinkling with mischief. "I find I can't be serious where you are concerned, my dear. You are far too lovely to be cooped up on this ship, and the ocean air doesn't sit well with your pallor. It should be much more ... rosy. I'm sure I could find a most pleasant way to make it so."

His eyes laughed at his teasing, but he didn't. If he were not such a scoundrel, he'd be too handsome by far, and half the time her foolish heart refused to overlook that fact. All he wanted was money. Her money. Her father had warned her about him before he'd even shown up at the wharf for departure. Shortly after they'd met for the first time in Father's drawing room, Father had told her that Abernathy had lost his family fortune a few years' past in London. He'd been in the states ever since, trying to win it back, without actually working. Marrying her would be a step in the right direction, but she'd been guarded with him from the first and that wouldn't change. It couldn't. But that didn't stop her from coming out to see if Abernathy would grace her with his presence almost every day.

There was also the chance that he didn't

want her money at all, but just the thrill of sparring with her until she gave in and let him into her room. He would lose, of course. She had no intention of giving herself to any man, much less Victor Abernathy, rake and gambling fiend.

Since her father would never let her marry a miner and she had no interest in marrying one, either, her prospects in the new little town would be slim—if her father was correct—and he always was. Blessings would be full of miners, and little else. That meant Lenora would remain alone until the little town became more settled, more civilized. She could wait that long and pray for someone who would make her think on her feet, like Mr. Abernathy did. He just had to be a man of character, who wouldn't chase after other women. That would never be tolerated.

"You have nothing to say?" He sighed and frowned dramatically. "Surely, in the long months we've spent together, I've convinced you there's more to me than just what's on the surface. What you can see, and hear, and ... touch."

He reached over and traced her finger with a practiced hand, meant to inflame her very skin. And it worked. His touch was as warm as apple pie and she prayed that Abernathy would tire of his games before he convinced her to believe he *had* changed. There was just no hope in that. But if he did tire of her, would she still come to the rail and hope? She refused to be another conquest for him, just another soft skirt. But where did that leave her? He wasn't bound to keep after her forever. He would tire of their talks and he would find another woman who gave him what he desired. A fleck of worry sparked within her.

"You have done no such thing. I remain certain that the only thing you wish from me is my father's money, and you shall never have it. Excuse me."

Lenora turned to leave his company, but his eyes caught her, and he moved in her path, stopping her like a bird in a cage. Though he did not touch her, she almost wished he would, just to know what it would be like to be held by him. That had to be how he'd tamed so many women; his beautiful, awful eyes, and the desire for his strong arms.

"I want more than your father's money, Lenora Farnsworth. I want your hand, and shall have it. I'm a gambler you see, and I never bet on a hand I might lose."

CHAPTER 2

San Francisco Port,
April 1851

Victor stood in the pressing crowd of bodies still aboard ship and watched as all four members of the Farnsworth family disembarked, his eyes naturally tracking the one they always did, the lovely Lenora. The Farnsworths were followed by two crewmen, each carrying a trunk. Great crowds of people rushed about the wharf below, and the ships that had arrived carrying people over the last two years sat bobbing nearby, now homes to those who couldn't afford housing on land. California was colorful and loud, just the place where he could fit in. There was an energy in the very air that made him feel like he was made of more than just the stuff God had willed together.

Victor had met Lenora's father, Edward Farnsworth, late September of 1850. After a short acquaintance, Mr. Farnsworth hired him to watch over he and his family on their trip to California. Victor had agreed, as long as Farnsworth hired his best mate, Cort Nelson, as well. Cort had gotten him out of more than a few tight places, and Victor wouldn't leave Cort behind. He was Victor's good luck charm and he'd need all the good luck he could find in California. Time was running out to replace the fortune he'd gambled away when it hadn't seemed to matter.

Lenora Farnsworth's hair blew softly in the breeze, catching both his eye and his breath. While he'd wiled away the hours with many an English maid, Lenora captivated something deep inside him, and it would not be quelled. The sky, temporarily dry, allowed her pretty, dark curls to create a luscious soft cloud around her beautiful face. Her skin was as fair as the driven snow and she was as dainty as a flower—and smart as a whip. She hadn't given in to him. Probably because she knew he'd take whatever he could. Her father would be furious if he knew Victor's plans for his daughter, but it would be worth it. Her soft pink lips and snapping blue eyes had haunted him from the moment he'd met her eight long months before.

Now, he'd need to follow the family to

Blessings, collect his pay, apply for a piece of land, and make his money, all so he could finally return home. With Lenora. He'd have to devise a plan for getting the gold back without spending it, but that was something he could work out later. Today, he just had to make sure the Farnsworths didn't leave without paying his fare, or Cort's.

Cort stood at his side, stiff, staring, his hands firmly on his irons, at the ready. He usually stayed hidden, liked it that way. He was a gun-slinger by trade, or so he said. Victor didn't know much about his past. He was wanted in Kentucky, for sure, but maybe other places, as well. So it was better that no one took notice of him.

"You don't think they'll skip out on paying for us? We can't get off this tea-kettle until he does, and it don't look like he's in any hurry."

Victor laid a calming hand on his friend's arm to stay him. He had no desire to rile Cort. That would be a bad idea, even for him. Cort had a way of getting under a man's skin, he wasn't a man to trifle with. Part of the reason he was good to keep around.

"He's trustworthy. He'll pay for our fare and then we'll do our jobs until they reach Blessings. He'll pay us then, and we can go. We are so close; can't you taste it?"

The gunslinger mumbled something Victor

was sure he didn't want to hear anyway.

Cort slid his hat a little lower. "And what if this town doesn't want us? They asked for Farnsworth. He didn't even tell Winslet he was bringing his family with him, so he don't know about us. And if he did, he'd never let us in."

Victor had already talked with Cort about that particular issue, and he was of a mind that it didn't matter. A town was a town and as long as he didn't make anyone too angry, they should be welcoming. There was enough gold in California for everyone, despite the rumors that the rush was already dying.

"Put your gun away for a while, Cort. Did you ever think about the fact that you could start over in Blessings? No one will know your past. You can be a new man."

"I already *am* a new man, new name and all. But that don't change my face or the fact that this whole world doesn't seem big enough to hide in anymore."

He couldn't argue that. The captain called their names and Victor and Cort made their way to the plank where they were verified, and the captain allowed them to leave ship. Edward Farnsworth, along with his wife Matilda, his son Geoff, and his beautiful daughter Lenora waited for them at the edge of the wharf as they secured some type of large cart to continue their journey. Though Lenora averted her eyes, she'd watched him approach. How one girl could seem so warm to him with her eyes and so cold with her mouth, was exciting. He'd make sure her mouth was good and warm to him eventually, too.

They had only been allowed a few trunks on the ship and neither he nor Cort had carried more than a bag. Mr. Farnsworth's eighteen-year-old son, Geoff, lifted their trunks into the back of the wagon. The trunks would be seating for the four who'd have to ride in the back. Geoff nodded to Victor, and made room for him to climb in at the end of the wagon. Victor had hoped on the outset of the voyage that by befriending the young man, he could get closer to his sister. That hadn't been the case. Geoff had turned out to dislike his parents a great deal, along with Lenora, and only tolerated Victor and Cort when he had to. Though, he was also an excellent card player, so the *friendship* wasn't for naught.

Victor pulled Mr. Farnsworth aside, his wife clinging to his arm as if she were about to be carted off by someone in the street. Since Farnsworth had insisted the family needed protection, he would use the advantage. He'd yet to see any real need for them to have been hired, but Farnsworth didn't see it that way.

Lenora had stolen Victor's every thought. Her quick wit, coupled with unmatched beauty, was like no other woman. He couldn't bear the thought of any other man near her, and he would make certain her father knew he cared for her.

"Mr. Farnsworth, I've asked around on the ship, the various men aboard, and they tell me that there are Indians outside the towns, just waiting to set upon unsuspecting travelers. That they will ravage the women and steal any goods worth taking in the wagons." It wasn't all a lie, some of the men said it, others had said the Indians were harmless, if left alone. Victor would do or say whatever was necessary to make sure Mr. Farnsworth took no chances.

Mrs. Farnsworth's eyes grew as big as marbles and she clutched her husband's arm. "Surely Cort will protect me and Mr. Abernathy will protect Lenora."

Mr. Farnsworth patted her hand absentmindedly. "We've spoken about my daughter. You know how I feel about the arrangement. Just make certain she is safe." He turned away to face his wife, then swung back around and stared Victor in the eyes. "Protect her, but that's as far as it goes. I have not given you permission for anything further."

He hadn't even expected for Farnsworth to agree to that much.

The family piled into the cart and Victor and Cort followed, Cort taking the seat next to Geoff, leaving Victor to sit next to Lenora. His thoughts immediately turned to the wicked. How he wanted that woman.

As he lowered himself onto the seat next to her, he felt her pull away, to move closer to the edge. He would not chase her this day, not with her father so close. He was not fond of fathers. They never seemed to approve of his methods, and he couldn't afford to perturb this one. Farnsworth owed him too much. If Victor hoped to get a lead on some good land, Farnsworth had to like him. So, he'd only speak to Lenora when no one was around to hear it. Lucky for him, or perhaps unfortunately, Lenora had a mind of her own and often found herself outside of her father's ever-watchful eye.

The driver cracked a long whip and the cart sprang forward. They slowly made their way through the flapping cotton jungle of San Francisco, the wealthiest poorhouse in the nation. Where a man would pay eight dollars to have his clothes washed, to return to a room that was little more than a wood framed tent. God Bless California.

After they'd left the ship, Father had quickly ushered them from the port, her mother weeping loudly. She couldn't be sure if it was due to the slave ship full of Oriental women, or if it

was her mother's fear of California that caused
it. The poor women were starved, mostly bare,
and on a stage for all to see. Lenora shuddered
as she remembered their vacant eyes.

Now that they were away from the wharf,
the very dirt itself seemed alive. She couldn't
focus on any one thing as the cart slowly
lumbered through San Francisco. On the water,
as they'd pulled to shore, the abandoned ships in
the harbor had bobbed like huge forgotten
flowers on a pond. Near the wharf, there had
been a great crush of bodies and busy activity,
too much for her to take in all at once. The lawns
of those who had invested well sat right next to
shacks made of little more than wishes and press
board. She'd never seen such strange hovels, not
even from the homeless in Boston. What awaited
them in Blessings?

"Father, how far is it?" The cart swayed to
the familiar rhythm, just as the ship, tamping
down a little of her excitement. At least they
were moving, making progress. Her father sat
next to the driver, with her mother on the end,
all of them tightly packed together on the bench
seat. The trunk she and Abernathy sat upon was
wedged behind the driver's bench. She craned
her neck up at her father, waiting for his answer.

When her father didn't reply, Mr. Abernathy
leaned in, his warm breath tickling the hair on
her neck and sending a pleasant heat through

her.

"It's at least a week, but don't fear. Cort and I are ready to protect you."

She ignored him and spoke louder; she'd yet to see any need for the protection they offered. "And will we have somewhere to live waiting for us?"

She'd never slept in a tent, and being so close to the elements would be difficult. It had been so rainy and damp that the road, with its deep ruts from wagons long gone, was about the consistency of mashed potatoes. The oxen struggled, and the wheels cut deeply into the road. Living in a tent would not only be difficult, it would be the worst part of the trip yet, with the possible exception of the Isthmus. There had been terrible bugs and sounds like she'd never heard before in the Panama jungle, not to mention the almost naked men that had pulled their boats down river to get them to the next waiting steamer. She shivered even now thinking about it.

Again, Abernathy answered her instead of her father. "There's most likely nothing there but tents. Your father will have to hire men, like me, to build you something quickly. He'll probably stop for lumber on the way, or at least for the tools. I've heard about the cost of goods here in California. It probably would've been better to cross over land, then you could've brought your own supplies. You'll pay three days' wages for a saw in California, mark my words."

She didn't want to mark his words or anything else about him. If her questions gave him the need to speak, she'd keep her mouth shut. He didn't need to know how vexed she was over him, how she should *not* want anything to do with him, yet needed to speak with him all the same. At least with her father sitting right at her back, she needn't worry about anything else he might say.

There would be no one else to speak to for a full week of riding. She'd be next to him, unable to escape his glances, or the discourse that forced her to consider every word. Her mother had little time for her, and since they had chosen to hire Abernathy and Cort, her brother Geoff had become distant as well. He never spoke to Father and Mother anymore, preferring to only talk to Cort, and only if he had to.

She tilted her head to avoid being caught staring. Cort—she didn't know his last name or if that was his name at all—would be nondescript in most settings. He didn't strike her as handsome or ghastly, he just *was*. In fact, it was his complete lack of discernible characteristics that made him compelling, her mind could forget his features almost immediately after glancing at something else. Rather, *someone* else.

Mr. Abernathy spoke quietly to Cort, and although they seemed to have no difficulty communicating, she couldn't make out a single word. Her brother gave their parents a quick glance, then pulled a deck of cards from his pocket.

"Anyone up for a deal?" he whispered.

Abernathy swiped the cards with a harsh growl and slid them in his pocket. "*Never* in front of a lady. There are women at card halls, but never ladies. It isn't something they need to know about."

The forbidden nature of the game made her curious, but she wouldn't ask. If Mother caught her watching a game of cards, she would be given more chores as a punishment. She was already carrying the load of her own and most of her mother's.

Geoff grumbled and leaned back in his seat in the bed of the wagon at their feet. "So, what do you two plan to do once we reach Blessings? I've a mind to convince Father to sell me a plot."

Cort shook his head, his face unreadable as always. "Don't be a fool. Your father will never give you a plot. If he did, he might be accused of being a cheat. If it's true that this Winslet needs your father to distribute the land, then you'll never see an ounce of it."

Geoff's eyes flashed, and he slid to the edge of the seat. "What do you know about it? Why even come to California if I can't try to strike like everyone else?"

The older man shrugged and laid down atop the trunks, covering his face with his hat.

Geoff wasn't ready to give up. "If he won't sell me a plot, then I'll just work with someone else. What about you Abernathy? You going to buy a plot?"

Lenora figured he would. How else could he make his quick money and return to his precious England where he could be with all the beautiful and alluring women he always spoke of? So beautiful that they put the sun to shame, he'd told her. Well, he could have them, every last one of them, and probably had, drat him!

Abernathy's firm jaw worked a little, as if he were chewing on his answer. "I'm going to try for a plot, but if I get one, I'd be sharing it with Cort. Your father might let you, it all depends on what's been surveyed. If all the plots have been surveyed, and they know there's gold on all of them, then he may let you, or not. It'll be up to Winslet. From what I've heard from your father, it all belongs to Winslet. Might also be that none of the plots have gold and Winslet is just looking to build a town."

The wheels creaked loudly as the oxen pulled them along. It had to be louder in the front where Father and Mother sat, as they'd ignored all attempts to speak to them. Though it could be that they were simply ignoring each other and, in so doing, missed all conversation around them. Father had made the decision to come, to sell the house and uproot the family. Mother hadn't wanted to. She had been far enough from her family while they'd lived in Boston, or so she'd claimed. Her family never visited, nor did they go to see her family. Now, she'd never have the opportunity to see them again. It had been eight months since Lenora's parents had been happy. She would never let California come between her and happiness, as it had for them.

Abernathy caught her hand for a moment and pressed it lightly, surprising her with his warm and gentle touch. "Miss Farnsworth, if you're tired from the ride, I would be happy to lay down a blanket on the floor of the wagon for you."

His familiarity sent heat racing to her cheeks, and all around inside her. "No, thank you." She drew her hand away from him, though she hadn't wanted to. "I am well." But her heart said she was anything but.

CHAPTER 3

San Francisco had been green, almost verdant, and Culloma was a welcome respite from the long drive, but the days in the back of the wagon grew tiresome. The constant drizzle meshed into one long trail of mud, damp, and inexhaustible attention from Abernathy. Lenora could barely turn around or find a quiet bush to use the necessary without the former Englishman following along. The day before, she'd reached the end of her patience and told him she'd rather be carried off by the Indians than have him provide her safety any further. It had only been a little lie. While the natives were terrifying, Mr. Abernathy had been relentless, and her poor confused heart didn't know how to deal with him.

As the old cart, now laden with building materials from Culloma, made its way slowly into the camp of Blessings, Lenora wanted to turn back. She'd held out hope that it was more like San Francisco, but it was just as many other mining towns, small, rustic, and muddy. Most of the actual structures were clapboard and hastily built, many were little more than tents. Her heart sank even lower. They would, again, be sleeping in the back of the cramped wagon. She tried not to complain, at least she was warm. Much *too* warm, pressed next to Mr. Abernathy, who had convinced her father that the natives would kidnap and ravage her if he didn't. She hadn't seen any Indians yet and suspected that Mr. Abernathy was just missing his usual bedmates. It also didn't help that she enjoyed his protective presence far too much.

The driver pulled up in front of a large home on the edge of town and her father climbed down from the cart.

"Atherton? You in there?" Father climbed the porch and knocked on the front door.

An older man with a long, white beard, friendly eyes, and a gap-toothed grin stepped from within and clapped her father on the shoulder. They spoke quietly for a moment, then approached the cart where her mother still sat, her back straight as a rod.

"Matilda, this is Atherton Winslet. He invited us to come to Blessings and help him set up the town."

Her mother gave a slight nod, but wouldn't come down.

Her father sighed slightly, then came to the back of the wagon. "Victor, Cort, if you're willing, I've got additional pay for you if you help me build the land office. We'll be living on the second floor."

While she had no doubt Cort had the strength to build a dwelling, Abernathy didn't seem to have the fortitude. Though he seemed strong, she doubted he'd lifted more than a hand of cards, or perhaps the hands of lovely women to his lips. Though, he hadn't done that to her since their first meeting. Abernathy narrowed his eyes and shared something conspiratorial with Cort, then nodded.

"It would depend on what you're offering. Now that we're here, Cort and I have to find a means to make a living."

Atherton heaved a dry laugh. "There's plenty of room to start what you'd like. Long as you've the gumption."

Abernathy tilted his head and caught her watching him. A wicked gleam sparked in his eyes. "The spirit is definitely willing."

Was he? Would he be willing to work to make the little town into something special as her father had envisioned? Or was Abernathy doing nothing more than twisting his words again?

Mr. Abernathy stood and climbed down from the wagon stiffly. He turned and offered her a hand. How she wished her father wasn't so absorbed in this Blessings business and would recall that he was her father, and that she still needed him to protect her from the likes of Victor Abernathy. Since hiring Abernathy for the job, he'd all but forgotten.

As her foot touched down on the muck in the street, Abernathy's hold tightened. "I do hope that I can secure employment quickly. I think you'll soon find that there is no better offer here, than mine."

Though his words made her heart do a little flip, and, while he might have spoken the truth, she'd never let him know it. Lenora slid her hand from his and held her hems out of the mud as she walked around him, creating the distance that needed to remain between them.

"You think rather highly of yourself, Mr. Abernathy. There may be wonderful men here, looking for a bride." And she would turn down every last one of them. Even this one. Because a gambling rake would never make a good husband.

"We're in California now, love. No need for drawing room conventions." He bowed low in mockery of his own words. "I am but Victor, your humble servant."

Words flowed from her tongue before she could bite them back. "I have great doubt you even know what humble means, Mr. Abernathy."

Lenora turned from a stunned Abernathy and followed her father and Mr. Winslet to a section of street just down from where the driver had parked the cart. The only thing in plentiful supply in the entire shanty town was mud; thick and soupy, suck her shoes into the mire, mud.

Lenora searched for a boardwalk or some place to set her feet where she wouldn't sink, and it was futile. Her mother called her back to the cart. As Lenora made her way back, her mother clutched the seat of the wagon with a grip that would rival any vice.

"Lenora, don't wander off too far without Mr. Abernathy or Mr. Cort. We don't know what sort of men live here." She glanced up and down the street, suspicion clouding her eyes and wrinkling a once clear forehead. "There might even be those Indians here," she whispered.

If the situation were humorous, she could almost laugh. There would be no wandering, and the street was so open that her mother could've seen anyone coming toward them. The town, as of the moment, was little more than a clearing that had the slight feel of a street, with a mercantile and saloon; more of a whisper of a street than an actuality.

Her mother's use of Cort's first name, as no one but her father seemed to know his last, was a testament to just how little her parents gave any attention to those they considered beneath them. Though there was hope for her father, her mother would never change.

Cort, Geoff, and Mr. Abernathy set to unloading the wood and the trunks as Mr. Winslet explained about Sheriff Pete Jones who watched over Blessings, and the four mines, and how it was safe to leave the building materials at the site. Lenora had little interest because it wasn't her home yet, nor would it be for some time.

Father turned around and took a deep breath, and a calm came over him she hadn't witnessed in months. "Do you smell that, Lenora? It's what peace smells like."

As she turned to take in the entire town, she took a deep breath. She'd wanted work, to prove her worth, to experience that same peace her father had. Blessings would certainly offer it. But at the moment, all she could smell, was the coming rain.

The cart slowly made its way out of town, heading back to San Francisco, the driver's pockets much heavier than they'd been a week before. Victor could've almost laughed at Lenora's petrified face. She'd assumed they would be sleeping in that cart until their home was built. She'd have to put up with a wet tent, just like everyone else who was new in the foundling town.

While Lenora was strong of will, Blessings would winnow her into a woman to be reckoned with, only making her all the more tempting. He would have to act fast before any other men in Blessings noticed her, for the men appeared to outnumber the women at least ten to one. Since there wouldn't be many women to pick from, he'd have to protect her from all of those men looking to wed. And in doing so, Blessings just might forge him, as well.

He'd spent every waking moment with her, keeping her safe, just as he'd promised her father. However, it had become the moments when they weren't supposed to be awake that had become a problem. Lenora was a soul-stirring beauty when awake, but softly reposed in sleep ... she was more exquisite than any dream he'd ever had, and no other man would ever see her like that. He'd stake his life on it.

She may defy him at every turn and spurn his very words, but while she slept, she admitted truths her mouth would deny during the light of day. She curled into him, nuzzled closer to him, sighed in her sleep. She was a sweet torment to him.

He found himself at her side, unable to stay away. "You thought the cart would stay?"

Her brow furrowed and her soft mouth pinched together, almost puckered, igniting a need he forced into submission.

"I was merely concerned with where we would all make our home until the office is built. Everything here is so damp."

"There will be some discomfort for a little while, but it will make you appreciate the basic home you'll have when we're finished building it. If you had gone right from the tight confines of the ship to a building ready-made, you would've turned up your pretty nose at it."

"You don't know me, Mr. Abernathy." She turned her face from him and he held back from pulling her toward him again.

"Oh, but I feel like I do. I remember well how you avoided your cabin the first few months at sea. It was so cramped and small compared to what you were used to. You felt trapped within the slight room. I saw you often at the rail of the ship. Then, later, when you were used to the confines of your room, you came out for *other reasons*." He couldn't keep from smiling. She'd found time to approach the rail and wait, casting a glance over her shoulder, always at him. She'd always left after he'd found her, as if she'd gotten just what she'd wanted, and after speaking to him, she could go about her day.

Her eyes were so blue they shocked him every time they sparked with anger, as they did just then, but he had to know why she'd sought out the most dangerous area of the ship, if not to see him?

"You assume that I came to the rail for you?" Her soft voice said he was treading into dangerous territory, fraught with current and undertow, but he had to know. He'd make her say it.

"I don't. Merely that you stopped mentioning the state of your cabin. Yet, even with the dangers of lascivious crewmen or being tossed overboard, you came out on the deck, nearly every single day."

Would she admit she craved his company, even a little? He ached to hear a word from her, anything that would let him know that his growing desire to be with only her, wasn't one-sided.

"The fresh air was preferable to mother's anger," she whispered, her eyes suddenly haunted, and he regretted his need immediately.

"I'm sorry to hear that, love." And he was. He'd never said more to a woman than he'd had to in order to get what he wanted, but Lenora was different. Nothing he knew of women had worked on her thus far, and he floundered with how to proceed. No amount of alluring talk or even teasing had changed her mind. But if a woman didn't want his charm, and he had no money to offer her, what then?

"I can't protect you from every hurt, Lenora. But at least I can keep you safe until your home is built. Cort and I will find a spot as dry as we can. You can count on me."

She raised her chin and her glassy eyes played havoc with him. He wanted to pull her close. Why did she fight him?

"Thank you, Mr. Abernathy."

His heart did a quick stutter, and he was left, mouth agape, as she walked away. It was the first word in kindness she'd spoken to him, and more addicting than a winning hand.

CHAPTER 4

True to his word, Victor had managed to find a spot a little higher than most of the town, with the exception of Winslet House, which sat on the top of a hill and looked out over Blessings. The area he'd found sat under a tall conifer tree; around the bottom was dirt, but drier than it was down in town. Her father had purchased a large canvas tent from Mr. Mosier at the mercantile, and they had set it up as one large room. Their beds were four slabs of wood on top of branches to keep them off the ground. Four. For the first time in a week, she'd be sleeping alone.

The first morning they had slept in the back of the wagon, she'd awoken to Victor's arm possessively around her middle, his body pressed to her back. She hadn't been sure if she should move his arm or just lay there and absorb him into her body. She could still hear his soft laughter in her ear, when he realized she was awake and just lying there.

"Did you enjoy waking up next to me as much as I did waking up next to you, love?"

He'd been awake, had known she hadn't moved his offending weight immediately and her insides had flamed with embarrassment. Yet, she couldn't deny how safe she'd felt there, nestled into him.

Victor and Cort had set up their own tent a little farther into the woods. Not far, but more distant than he'd been in a long time. Good, at least she could fall asleep without worrying if he would do something untoward. Not that her father had seemed at all perturbed by Victor and his actions. He had, in fact, seemed to almost push her to spend more time with the prodigal Englishman.

She pushed herself from her wooden slab and stretched her sore back. The tent was dark with the trees shading it, and at least it was somewhat dry. There was little else to say about it. Something clanged together just outside, followed by muffled angry words.

Her mother strode in, grumbling about the damp and the beds, the cooking stove that wasn't hooked up yet, and the town that *wasn't* a town at all. Matilda Farnsworth had been a housewife in Boston with little more to do than raise her children and volunteer where she'd chosen, and her choices had always been genteel. She'd read French poetry to the men at the veteran's home and knit socks for orphans, but she'd never gone to see them. She'd never actually touched a single veteran or helped them with a practical need, just sat on her chair and read her few pages.

Blessings would never be a home for her mother. Matilda didn't understand the provocative desire to build something and make it, form it, work until it came to its ultimate fruition. That was what drove Lenora to put up with eight long months in a boat that made her ill, the mud that clung to everything, and the miners. In Blessings, she could be somebody, instead of just *anybody*.

"Lenora, stop gawking at this horrid place and help me." Mother held up a rabbit with dainty pinched fingers. It needed to be skinned and prepared, and Mother's pallor went quite gray. "Mr. Winslet was *kind* enough to provide us with our supper."

Lenora almost laughed. Almost. She knew even less about cooking than her mother, the only thing that made her own cooking palatable was that she wanted to learn. She'd found early on in their travels that the way to learn was from someone who knew, not Mother. Just about any other woman alive would know more than Mother. There was a tent a little farther back, she'd heard a woman singing. The Winslet's were all the way across the clearing in a two-story house on a little rise above Blessings, but that tent couldn't be far, not if she'd heard them. Chances were good that where there was a woman, she would find someone who knew what to do with the rabbit.

"Do you know how to prepare that?" Lenora opened her mother's trunk where they kept their two cooking pots.

"Cook it? I don't even know how to get the fur off."

Lenora held out the pan and her mother laid the animal in it, then collapsed onto her bed plank.

"I can't do this. He expects too much of me."

It was her father's job to lead the family and he'd led them to California. He'd done it for the good of all of them, and for the little town he'd loved the moment he heard about it. There would be no turning back. Either Mother had to learn to live in Blessings, or she'd have to learn to live in unhappiness.

"Rest for a moment, Mother. I'll go find out how to cook this."

Her mother seemed more distraught by the

day, and Lenora prayed that she wouldn't run off. There didn't seem to be any easy way to leave Blessings. One of the few ways would be with Mr. Mosier. he made supply runs every three weeks or so for the mercantile, according to her father. But he would never agree to split up a family. Not that she would want it to be split, but Mother had always been unhappy, even in Boston.

As Lenora left the tent and wandered up the hill to where she'd heard the voice earlier, the trees seemed to close in around her, and the area darkened. A woman, with pure pale skin and amber eyes like a cat's, peered out at her from behind a tree. Her red cloak with a large hood hid most of her. Lenora stood transfixed as the woman approached and slid her hood down, revealing hair like a raven's, with a red flower tucked behind her ear.

The woman plucked the flower from its perch and handed it to Lenora. "Here, to ward off the dark," she said softly, in French.

Lenora had never been more thankful for her mother's drawing room instruction of all the things she'd considered useless, including the French lessons. The flower did seem to brighten everything dark around the very small clearing surrounded by tall redwoods. The trees seemed to hang less close, the dark less powerful.

"Wait!" Lenora called, forgetting her French

momentarily as the woman walked back to her fire.

The woman turned around and gave her a questioning glance and Lenora searched her memories for how to ask just what she needed to. When was the last time she'd ever used any of that French her mother had tried to engrain into her very thoughts?

"We are new here and I don't know how to cook rabbit. *S'il vous plait?*"

She held out the rabbit, still laying limply inside the cast iron Dutch oven. Though she'd learned for years, she'd never took the time to practice her French as she should've, and the word for cooking pot had completely slipped from her mind ... if it had ever been there to begin with.

The woman smiled softly and glanced to her fire, but did not answer. If not from this woman, where could she learn? Cort had helped her prepare meals some along the trail, but he was not friendly to her. The woman cast her one more glance, gasped, flipped her hood back in place, and dashed into her tent as strong hands gripped Lenora's shoulders and turned her around, her heart suddenly hammering against her stays.

"Come, love. You've ventured too far into the forest." Victor's voice immediately calmed her sudden fright, then inflamed her anger. She stepped closer to him, knocking his hands off her.

"I was never told that I couldn't venture to see my neighbors, Mr. Abernathy. You've frightened her away!"

The heat from his glance put the spark of the fire a few yards away to shame. Was he angry with her? He'd never shown her anything but his playful banter. There was more to Mr. Abernathy than she'd suspected, and his emotion drew her ever nearer.

"You *will* give in eventually and call me Victor, yes?" His voice held a waver he'd never let show before. She'd scared him by venturing out into the forest. He stepped within a breath of her, and her heart raced even faster.

Though the woman had been a stranger to her, Lenora hadn't felt a sliver of fear in her presence, but Victor made her quiver as if she'd run the whole way. He wouldn't do anything to harm her, but the anger in his eyes was slowly melting to something a sight needier, but just as hot.

"I don't think it would be prudent to encourage you, Mr. Abernathy. You already seem to feel you can take liberties whenever you like."

The burn of his eyes intensified as his gaze slipped to her lips, telling her just where he'd take those liberties if she'd let him.

He lowered his voice to just above a whisper. "I shall miss you pressed against me tonight, love."

Would he ever stop calling her that? Her body shuddered before she could stop the action. His words were like a caress, and her mind ached for it just as much as her skin did.

If her father could only hear the true Victor Abernathy, he'd never let her out of his sight, yet she couldn't deny that she'd slept better the last week than she had since they'd left Boston. The hard, wooden slab of her cot left little appeal. During those long nights in the wagon, Victor's strength pressed alongside her had given her a feeling of safety she couldn't explain.

"I'm sure if you left your gun with me so that I might still protect myself, I would sleep just as well."

Never would she admit to him that he was anything to her, that she was ever-slowly growing to enjoy his attention, to crave it. Lord help her, because He couldn't possibly want her to fall for such a man. Victor would make his money and return to England, leaving her alone and lonely. She would never offer to go anywhere again, so following him back to England was out of the question, not that he would ever want her to. She was just another conquest for Victor, someone he could talk about to lure the next woman that caught his eye. She could never allow herself to be anything more to Victor than the daughter of the man who hired him.

He reached for her elbow and gently drew her back down the hill toward her tent. As she'd thought, her mother had not yet built a fire. There was no smoke or flame to be seen. Lenora prayed the rabbit would cook quickly, once she figured out how to skin and prepare it. One thing was certain, the gambling Englishman wouldn't know what to do with it. Once they'd reached her tent, he tipped his bowler, which was now quite dirty and used, and left.

Kindling sat just inside the tent, and she soon had a good fire going, but it was difficult to focus on preparing the meal when she could think of nothing beyond Victor and his response to the cloaked woman. The woman from the wood's bright golden eyes were hauntingly beautiful, but there was something strange about her as well, something unknown. Victor's warning about not traveling too far into the forest had just the effect he'd intended to keep her out of the forest. She was terrified. Her skin prickled with every twig snap or voice floating from town. There would be no protective Englishman by her cot that night.

After only three days, the new Farnsworth Land and Law Office was complete. While the town employed about fifty men, when they were needed, they all turned up to help build. Victor stood across the area that would pass for a street and gave the two-story building an appraisal. Though he knew it was put together as well as it could be, it seemed to lean, standing there all on its own, like a good stiff wind would knock it right over. Blessings needed more buildings, more business. But he wouldn't be there to see it.

Cort met him and propped himself up on his shovel. "So, it's done. Our time of working for Farnsworth is over. Now you can forget about that dark-haired curiosity and start thinking about what you're going to do to get home. She's been a distraction for you."

Victor widened his stance and stared at the building for a moment. He'd personally worked on the rooms upstairs and his Lenora would sleep in one of them, at least for a time, until he convinced her that she needed to be with him.

"She isn't just a distraction, Cort. She's in my blood and it would be just as hard to give her up as that which flows through my veins. I'm a man engulfed."

He smiled, Cort would never understand. His gun and his secrecy were his mistresses, and they were a jealous lot.

"She's a woman. Just because there are so few here, doesn't mean you have to attach yourself to one of them. I think it would be best for you if you just walked away. Let that one be, or you'll be in Blessings for the rest of your life."

There were other women; Ellie, the owner of the Saloon; the strange woman he'd caught Lenora speaking with three days before, and a few others who were married.

Everyone he'd spoken to had warned him of the cat-eyed witch in the forest. He hadn't believed it, miners could be superstitious, but the very look of her was mysterious, and he'd needed to get Lenora away. The necessity to protect her in the wilderness was strong, and now that she wouldn't be close by, he ached to pitch his tent by her front door and do the job anyway. It was as if the Lord Himself had laid the job on his heart, because he couldn't stop himself.

"She isn't just any woman. You might know your horses, Cort, but leave the women to me."

Cort glanced up and down the street, seemingly alert for coming dangers. Old habits were hard to break, and the fact that Cort couldn't just relax was unsettling.

"Now that you don't need to *act*, we need to figure out how we'll get a job at one of the mines, get our plot for housing, and get started. There's ample wood around here that will need to be cleared, and we can build a small house."

There were a few trees in the area, but it mattered little to him if they just stayed in the tent. Get rich and get out. That was his plan.

Cort scratched his stubbly jaw. "Let's get the go-ahead from Winslet, then we'll see what we need."

Victor had gone from a landowner in England, who gambled everything away, to a dirt sifting miner—or at least he would once he got the job. He could almost laugh. They might eventually make money, if Blessings held the gold Winslet claimed, but he didn't have long. He'd have to get another letter out to his mother now that he'd found a place to stop and find out just what had happened with his parents. It had been almost a year since he'd sent them a letter and if they'd replied to Boston, he'd never see it.

"I can see this town growing. It's a good spot." Victor said, without commitment, because he still wouldn't offer to stay. He just needed his money and to whisk Lenora off her feet and back to England. Victor turned his attention from the land office to Cort.

Cort had an unfamiliar glint in his eye, almost happiness. "Yup. Good place for this man to start over. No one's looking for me in California. If we make a little money in the mines, I may just put down roots here. Maybe I should start looking for a woman." Cort choked on a laugh.

"I've been wandering with you for over three years, Cort. I didn't even know you looked at women." He laughed. Cort had about as much humor as a mama grizzly with a cub.

"I know a pretty woman when I see one. Your gal, she just don't quite fit me."

The insinuation that Lenora was lacking angered him, but better that Cort not look at all. While he doubted the miners, who kept to themselves for the most part, would interest Lenora, Cort was close in age and at least educated enough that he could read. He was the only other competition at the moment.

"Let's stop worrying over the lack of femininity here in Blessings, for now, and see about getting a job."

Cort nodded, a strange smile wandered over his face and was gone in an instant. "You don't think I'll die alone, do you?"

Victor clapped him on the back. His only friend tended to get melancholia rather easily. "Nope. As long as you can keep from swinging at the end of a rope. I think, if you stay here, love will find you."

CHAPTER 5

Soft voices rose up the stairs as Lenora readied herself for her first day of working with her father. Before they'd left Boston, he'd promised that she could learn from him and help in the office, giving her something to do. There was no telling if he remembered his promise until she went down and asked him. She pushed the last pin in her hair and wandered to the staircase to listen.

Her father spoke to a man, but she didn't recognize the voice. Not surprising, since it could be any number of men from the small town, or even her brother. And the voices were so muffled, she couldn't even tell which was her father.

Mother turned from the stove and pursed her lips. "Just where do you think you're going? You've got no business wandering about town, especially now that Cort and Victor have other duties."

And good riddance...

She wanted to believe that, but the more he wheedled, the easier it was to listen to the cravings of her wicked heart. "I was only going down to the office. Father said that I might assist him."

How she'd dreamed of becoming a lawyer like her father. Geoff had never expressed interest. If they had remained in Boston, she would've petitioned Father to go to law school. There was no way to know if California held any schools that would allow a woman to learn, but if there was, she prayed her father would see her desire and send her.

"And just where does that leave your brother? If anyone should be helping your father with his business, it should be Geoff, not you."

She hated to point out that her brother was so angry about father's choice to hire Victor and Cort, instead of relying on his own son for protection, it had caused a rift that would be difficult to bridge. Geoff's pride had been sorely hurt. But it would do little good to say anything. Mother would never believe it, anyway.

"Geoff is out of the house, so if Father wants

help, he'll have to settle for me. If Father should change his mind, I'll do as he asks." At least for a day. Geoff wasn't ready to sit and work through more than a few hours. His temper had taken over and he was often gone from them for days at a time. Not to mention, Mother wouldn't argue outright with anything Father had said, so Lenora would be allowed to work, for now.

Her mother had learned how to cook since arriving in California. But even after a few weeks cooking by the fire, she was still preparing food that was suspect. It just further drove home the truth further, that her mother couldn't possibly be hiding the secrets the *respected* people of Boston said of her. She had suffered humiliating taunts for her tightly curled black hair, dark as coffee eyes, and skin that had just a hint of olive tone. Lenora had always doubted the rumors because her mother was privy to knowledge that a slave would not have; classic literature and French, and nothing of the domestic, such as cooking.

It had been rumored that Mother was descended from a house slave who'd pleased her master. As far as Lenora knew, it was all lies, but her mother never spoke about her heritage. The family her mother had fought to stay close to, had never bothered to show up in Boston, nor had they ever gone to visit. Lenora had never met her aunts or uncles, not even her grandparents on her mother's side of the family.

Lenora herself had her mother's thick, dark, curly hair, and her father's bright blue eyes. Since she was a child, she'd been told that she was striking, but looks were just something that would fade, her mind would not. She was capable and would prove it.

The thin boards of the stairs creaked under her as she tried to quietly descend them. Interrupting father during business would be a mark against her. As she reached the bottom and finally tore her glance from her feet, Victor Abernathy stood talking with her father. He smiled at her and when her father turned away from Victor to greet her, Victor had the audacity to wink, the cad.

Her father approached her, and she put on a smile for him. "Good morning, Father. I've come down to assist you. Perhaps you could show me the work you do with Mr. Abernathy?"

Victor's eyes twinkled at her and she made it a point to avoid his gaze further.

"I would love to, dear, but I won't be granting Mr. Abernathy a plot, at least not until he can secure a position at the mine. We've discussed it already and the rumors surrounding the reason he is in America are enough that I simply can't trust him with a building plot until he can prove to Mr. Winslet that he intends to stay. People come to Blessings to build a future, not to strike it rich and leave. Isn't that right, Mr. Abernathy?"

Her father chose that moment to glance back at Victor, as did she. His lips were set in a perturbed line, and the tension that poured from him was palpable. She wanted to leave before some of that coiled energy unleashed. Her heart ached for him; he was away from his family and now unable to work the mine or have a plot of his own.

During their time together on the steamer and in the wagon, he'd boasted to her that he would get a plot, find gold, and make an offer for her hand, all within the span of three weeks. Without her father's help, that seemed rather unlikely.

"I will find work and I will prove to you that I'm trustworthy, Mr. Farnsworth." He donned his hat, nodded to her, and was gone.

She almost felt sorry for him. It came back in a rush, all those times her friends were invited to parties, and her family was not. Slaves weren't welcome. It never mattered how successful Father was, it never stopped the talk. Lenora had grown to hate it all, which was why she was yet unmarried. She'd refused to even see any man whose family had spited them because of the lies about her mother.

"Father, with all the talk that went on in Boston about Mother, talk that we know to be

false, is it fair to judge Mr. Abernathy based
solely on rumor?"

Her father smiled at her and flipped open
his huge ledger. "I'm not the only one who's
judged him based on innuendo, my dear. You've
heard things about him as well, things from the
ship that a lady would never talk about. I know
you've heard them because I can see the way you
look at him, with questions in your eyes. You're
far too honest. It's good that we got you away
from Boston when we did, or that trait would've
landed us in trouble. The higher the society, the
more secrets it keeps."

She hated that he was trying to change the
subject. In this one thing, she could help Victor
without him ever knowing.

"Are you saying that what I heard was a lie?"
She wouldn't believe it even if Father told her.
Not only had he been the one to tell her, she'd
seen him talking to other women. He'd done it
right in front of her, often glancing at her to see
if she'd taken notice, and laughing heartily when
he caught her. Victor was a scoundrel, a rogue,
her mother would call him a rake, and that was
probably the closest to the truth. Yet her heart
wouldn't listen, it wanted his company all the
same.

"Mr. Abernathy and I have had occasion to
have a few long talks, Lenora. I may not trust
him with Mr. Winslet's precious land because of

the stipulations he's put on it." He slipped a gentle finger under her chin and lifted her face to look into his blue, honest eyes. "But I do trust him to protect my only daughter. So, now you know the truth."

Count your blessings... His mother had always said it. She'd tried to let him be, to grow up without much direction, other than the glib remarks and platitudes. He'd thumbed his nose at all of it, convinced that the money, drinks, and women would never run dry. Until, one day they did. His father had sat him down in his study and shown him the ledger from the estate. The huge book was full of figures and every last one of them was bleak.

Five years later, and he hadn't heard a word from home. Did his family still own the estate? Was he still entitled to anything? The rumor that he was there to earn back his fortune was only partially true. When his father had shown Victor what his behavior had cost the family, he'd left to avoid further shame. Before he'd left, his mother had suggested he try to recapture the fortune in America. Now, he knew nothing, except that she was waiting for him to return home, hopeful he would bring the money to pay off his debt to the family. Yet his father's parting glare of shame sat with him all five years. He couldn't go home empty-handed. When he returned, they would tell him if he might inherit anything. How rich; to inherit what he had to earn.

Now, he saw that life for what it had been, empty. The Farnsworths were a family. They didn't love each other more or less than anyone else, but they still had what he could no longer claim; family, heritage, a place to belong.

Though his newly acquired *wealth* was small, it was still more than he'd earned for years trying various things in Boston—cards more than anything. He'd get good on one gambling boat and then they'd accuse him of cheating, take his winnings or whatever he had on him, and forcibly remove him. He wasn't a cheat, but they didn't like winners. It was bad for their business.

He'd met Cort when they'd both been thrown off the same boat, Luck's Lady, for different reasons. Together, they'd gotten good and sloppy on cheap bourbon, and Cort had shared the story of his life after Victor had shared his. They'd become like brothers after that. If Victor went back to England, Cort would have to come with him. Then his friend could finally be free of the demons that chased him.

Victor and Cort had agreed that morning over the cook fire that they needed a plot, and that Victor was more likely to get it, since he'd been the closest with Mr. Farnsworth. Now they had no options; Winslet had said no. Because the town was so fledgling, there weren't many businesses to find work. They'd have to start something new. He could offer his building skills, after helping Mr. Farnsworth raise his business and home. But that had been a lot more strenuous than he'd expected.

Along the path, heading back to a small area he and Cort had claimed for their tent on the opposite end of town as Winslet House, Cort slid from behind one of the many trees and joined him. How Cort always knew where he'd be was an absolute mystery.

"Did you get us some land?" he said, without preamble.

"No, sorry. He doesn't believe we'll stay and help the town prosper. Winslet said he couldn't grant plots to anyone who wasn't hired by the mine, and when I met with Winslet earlier he said he wouldn't hire me because he doesn't think I'll stay."

Cort laughed dryly. "He's rather astute. You *didn't* plan to stay here or reinvest what you find in the town, you were going to find it and head out."

It was only partially true. "Wrong, I was going to find it, ask for Farnsworth's daughter's hand, take her whether he agreed or not, and *then* leave."

"So, what now?"

Cort ignored his ignoble plan. He most likely had an idea of his own, he always did, but he generally left Victor the job of suggesting it first.

"You said you ran horses for a while, in Kentucky?"

Cort narrowed his eyes and glanced behind them. "*I* didn't run horses. *Hayes* knew a few men in the horse business."

"Nelson, Hayes, it's no matter. You know horses, right?"

"If you want me to be here to help you, you'll bury that name and that past deep in your memory and not take it out again."

Cort could be temperamental, but he was the best shot Victor had ever seen, and he wasn't about to lose the firepower over a spat.

"Fine. Cort, do you know horses? I think we could start a livery. It's about the only thing either of us know."

"And by that, you mean you want me to run it."

The man wasn't stupid, Victor knew a good horse when he saw one, could saddle it if a groom wasn't available, and might be able to pitch fodder, but his knowledge was limited.

"Of course."

Cort shook his head and spat, taking his time to answer. "You don't think there's any other way? Opening up a business ties us here, both of us. I'm not leaving once we invest in something that big, and I won't let you, either."

That was the plan. Make old Winslet think they'd changed their ways and were ready to settle down. It meant he'd have to let Cort stay behind, and lie to him for the very first time, but if he had to, he would.

"Exactly. After a few weeks, they'll let me have that job in the mines, and I can get us a house plot because we've invested in this little town. And then I'll do just as we planned."

"Except you forgot one thing. If we buy what we need to start the livery, there won't be any left to rent the plot. We'll have to work for it."

The longer he had to work, the harder it would be to stay away from Miss Farnsworth, and he'd never had to wait this long for a woman. He'd needed to get his money quickly, so he could sweep her right back to the bay and off to England, to his waiting family. His mother wouldn't find a single fault with her, *he* certainly couldn't.

"We already managed to build the law office, and just downstream, they are working on the mill. It'll be ready soon. We could work on cutting timber this week and, with help from a few men in town, have the livery up and running in five to seven days. Farnsworth would let us use his tools. He won't ever use them again."

"Culloma is out of the question. Everything

was far too expensive. They charged a dollar for a glass of milk, and it was watered down by half," Cort grumbled.

"That's your penance for drinking the stuff." Even the thought of milk curled his insides, but to Cort, it was something he called *home-food.*

Victor wouldn't give up a single cent that he didn't have to, but there also might be a way to earn some of their money back a bit quicker. "I have another way we can earn a little money, same as we did before we got here. We'll pull up our tent and move it out into the forest, but let a few select miners know that there will be cards every night. High stakes, not like the saloon."

Victor couldn't believe he hadn't thought of it sooner. The quicker he and Cort fleeced the good miners of their earnings, the quicker he could be on his way.

"You know that Geoff will be down there every night and it'll only be a matter of time before Mr. Farnsworth finds out. You may be in his good graces when it comes to his daughter now, but if you bring gambling into Blessings, be prepared to deal with the consequences."

Farnsworth might get angry, but it would be Winslet he'd have to worry about. Winslet held the cards in Blessings, and he was sitting on a full house.

CHAPTER 6

Edward Farnsworth was a hard man to please, but Lenora couldn't stop thinking about all the things she'd learned as she walked a sample down to the Winslet Mine office. So far, she'd managed to stay out of her father's way and learn more than she'd thought possible. She now knew how to accept the gold samples from the prospectors, and to label them accordingly, and her father had even trusted her to take them over to Mr. Winslet—he was such a hoot. She now knew the land around Blessings so well that, when someone spoke about the section numbers the miners gave, she knew just where they were talking about.

Mr. Winslet sat in his office, his old boots

propped up on his desk that looked suspiciously like old crates, but she'd never asked him about them.

"Afternoon, Miss Farnsworth. Have you brought me more dirt?" His eyes twinkled. He'd teased her the first time she'd brought a sample, as it'd had almost no 'color' at all.

"Yes, sir. A fine sample from near the east mine, section five."

He nodded and slapped the sample on the corner of his desk. She wasn't privy to what he did with them after she brought them.

"Your father is proud of you, you know." His hazel eyes seemed to look right into her soul. Her father had said that Winslet had an uncanny ability to know a man, without knowing him at all.

"That remains to be seen. He's yet to trust me with any more important task than bringing you bottles of dirt." Though she prayed there was something more in them, for Mr. Winslet's sake.

"Just because he don't do what you expect him to, don't mean that he ain't proud. He wouldn't be workin' so hard to teach you iff'n he weren't."

She'd had to try so hard just to get Father to agree to let her work with him that it didn't seem possible.

"Thank you, sir." She turned, trying to avoid

more conversation as Millie Winslet walked in.

"Lenora! So good to see you. Were you able to make use of that hare?" Millie smiled and wrapped an arm about her shoulders. "I haven't seen your mother since the land office was built, tell her she needs to come over and have a sit."

Her mother hadn't left the house, and had taken to cowering in her room, but Father wouldn't approve of her telling anyone, especially the town founder and his wife. They might feel responsible, and Lenora knew it wasn't the Winslet's fault in the slightest.

"The hare was delicious, thank you." And surprisingly, it had been. Once she'd figured out it had to be skinned like a chicken, the rest had been easy. "She's been feeling poorly. Please don't take it as a slight."

Millie nodded and released her hold on Lenora's shoulders. The loss was immediate, her own mother had never been the type to give such attention.

"As soon as she's up to it, come on over and I'll show you how to make rabbit that'll melt in your mouth."

"Oh!" Mr. Winslet jumped to his feet. "I almost forgot. You dropped these when you were in here the other day." His smile caught her heart as he dropped two coins in her palm.

"I did no such thing." She hated taking his money when her own father wouldn't pay her.

"Oh, I'm certain they're yours." He shooed her toward the door. "Your father is waitin' on you, best get back to work."

"Thank you, sir." She slipped the coins into her pocket and vowed to save them.

Back at the office, she sighed and slid onto her hard, wooden stool. The whole room was the same size as their home, but her father had wanted her desk away from his. It sat near the front window, so she could see when people were going to come in and could welcome them. Though, her gaze seemed to look for one man more than others, the one man she kept telling herself she had to avoid, and who shouldn't be coming in anyway, since he wouldn't be getting a plot.

Good girls did not fall for rakes. She had to keep telling herself that, or be lost forever.

Her father hadn't seen much need for her at first, but she'd soon shown him that someone who could dictate messages, keep a tidy office, and follow orders was an asset. Despite all the work she'd done, he'd yet to pay her a cent. Mr. Winslet, in his own wily way, had made sure that she had a few coins in her pocket for delivering things for him, but her own father saw little need to pay her.

As he'd done every day since she started, Victor sauntered by, catching her glance in the window before he ever opened the door. He always seemed to sense when she was about to look up and then he would act as if he'd been standing there for years, smile with one of his lady-tripping smiles, and completely upend her work for as long as he was present.

Victor ambled in the door and flung his hat onto her desk with a leisurely air, just atop all her papers. He'd had it cleaned, or purchased a new one.

"Are you keeping busy, love?" His eyes twinkled at her.

How had he known—for he always knew—when her father was out and he could speak plainly with her? His suit had been freshly laundered and repaired to match his hat. After seeing him for so long with his stained and worn suits, he was far too dashing now. She couldn't keep herself from taking him in, top to toe.

"Yes, Mr. Abernathy. Father keeps me quite busy. Was there something I could do for you?" Since he couldn't be there for land reasons.

She regretted the words before they left her lips. A smile spread across his face, so handsome, but a little frightening in its utter honesty and desire. For her.

"Why, you know there is. You could accept my proposal. You only have a week before the time I set runs out and you'll accept anyway."

His three-week time frame may have been a sealed deal in his mind, but it was far from finished in hers. Why he persisted in pestering her for a hand he wouldn't want to keep, eluded her.

"Mr. Abernathy, I will not be accepting the suit of you, or any other man. I have work with my father now, and a long life ahead of me, helping this little town grow. It will be great, you know. You'll never see it if you move back to London to be with all those beautiful women you talked about on the journey here."

A twinge of regret hit the back of her heart harder than she expected. There would be no one for her to talk to in all of Blessings once he was gone. For as kind and wonderful as Millie Winslet was, she wasn't a friend and no one else had made her acquaintance. Victor stepped closer to her desk, lingering over her. Her heart raced as his firm mouth quirked just a bit. Did he always have to be so in control?

"You think I want anything to do with those frivolous ninnies after I've had eight months to watch you, to think of nothing but you? You think for a moment that I could settle for little more than a pretty skirt when I could have someone who will challenge me daily? Do you, Lenora?"

Oh, how she ached to believe him. If he'd ever used her given name before, she'd thoroughly missed it, and with his slight accent, the sound of it on his lips gave her heart a sweet stutter. So much so that she could hardly think of the words she should say.

"I know nothing of your English women, only what you've said of them."

She folded her hands in her lap to hide the disquiet in her very soul. "Since I cannot sell you what you ask for ... good day, Mr. Abernathy."

He leaned down low, until his cheek was next to hers. So close that if he'd had whiskers, she would've felt them. The heat from him poured over her body, yet she shivered.

"I don't come in here every day for the land, love. Ten more days."

He slipped his hat off her papers and donned it as he slid out the door, leaving her completely out of sorts, as usual. Her father came in through the back, shaking his head.

"I wish people would leave well enough alone," he muttered.

Lenora backed out of her chair and mentally shook off the faltering of her heart. She stood as a sign of respect to her father, but his mutterings were also curious.

"Is someone meddling in your business, Father?"

There was most likely nothing more she could do than listen. Her father had been very weary lately. Mother wanted nothing to do with Blessings, or the family, and had threatened to leave if he didn't do something quickly. No one had any idea what could be done to make it more hospitable for her, so most of the evenings were spent avoiding her and her temper.

"There are a few miners convinced that one of the other miners is housing a witch. I've told those worried to just leave her and her brother be, since they are quiet and not hurting anyone, but people are scared."

The woman in the woods came immediately to mind, especially after Victor's concern over her wandering into the woods. The woman had seemed so kind, yet, there was an air of the mysterious about her.

"A witch? How do they know?"

"She wears a cape that covers her in all weather, even when it's blistering hot, not just a bonnet. She collects plants and when she speaks, no one can understand her. When she does speak, they say it sounds like song. They think she's cursing them. But what most people mention, are her eyes. Like a cat's, they say. I've yet to meet the woman or her brother because they keep to themselves. That may have done more harm than good."

Her father would understand rumors, people had talked about her mother behind her back as well. The poor woman was probably lonely. "Father, it isn't curses. She speaks French. I met her when we first got here."

He rested a large hand on her shoulder and

his tired eyes gazed into hers for a moment. "You'd best stay away. I don't believe the nonsense, but our reputation is at stake. People here need to trust us. I can't control you, and I won't. You're a capable young woman, but having this job also means you must think of me and my reputation at all times, even above your own."

A reputation that could be easily tarnished. If Mr. Abernathy continued to come in when her father was out, and continued pestering her for her hand, she could risk hurting her father's business. There had to be a way to deter him, keep him busy so he could give her a few days' peace.

"Have you granted Mr. Abernathy and Mr...," she'd only just learned that Cort had a surname, " ...Nelson, the land to build the livery?" Everyone had called him Mr. Cort for the entire journey.

Her father turned and made his way to his desk, completely covered with paperwork, at the back of the office. "Yes, just yesterday. Mr. Winslet wanted the plot well away from Blessings proper and far away from any of the mines, lest Abernathy had ideas about using his plot for digging instead of building. I was going to finish the papers and deliver them to him later. But, I think that might be a good job for my assistant." He glanced up at her and, for a moment, his warm old smile was back in place.

"I don't think that's such a good idea. What would people think of me, visiting the tent of two single men?" Not to mention she wasn't even sure where they camped now that she wasn't living in a tent near him. He had to still be out there, but had he moved now that he wasn't needed?

Her father sat down in his chair and moved some papers around. "I should be done with this within the hour. Finish up whatever you're doing, then you can deliver this. The men are expecting it. You can find them at section 37."

She knew better than to test her father when he gave an order, while her belly was alight with pleasant excitement at the idea of seeking Victor out. And this time, she wouldn't have to pretend she wasn't.

In Blessings, a man could throw away his razor, or so Mr. Atherton, the friendly benefactor of the entire town would always say, but not Victor. At least, not yet. He scratched his chin, still hot from the morning's ministrations. But, it wasn't as hot as his blood. Cort would claim it was just because it had been too long since he'd spent an evening with a fine woman, but he couldn't even think of any other anymore.

Blessings had no such establishment, even if he could consider such a thing. But he couldn't, none other would do. Only Lenora. He wanted those blue eyes to snap at him with both fury and passion, in equal measure.

But that wouldn't happen without a plot. He'd have to think of another option now that Winslet had turned him down. How could he be good enough to court Farnsworth's daughter, but not good enough to mine for gold? Farnsworth had given him permission, if not outright approval to ask his daughter for her hand when the time came, as long as she was amenable to it. She would be if he could just keep seeing her, keep pushing his advantages, play his hand right.

As he approached the humble tent where he and Cort had set up home, Cort raised a tin cup to him with an offering of coffee. They didn't have much of anything. A few cups, two plates, one pot, and lots of other makeshift equipment. They had fashioned a hanger for their cook pot out of three sticks and a bit of hemp rope because they could find no chain. So far, the handle had resisted burning the rope too extensively. Their seating was no more than two large rounds of wood.

"Thank you." Victor was happy for the brew. At least he hadn't been the one to have to make it. Cort was better at that sort of thing. Victor never had to cook, and even now would settle for travel rations before he'd try cooking anything.

He slid his coat off and threw it onto his pallet to keep it from the mud, and sat on a stump alongside Cort. Cort had a lot on his mind that morning, if the intense look in his eye was any indication.

"You went to the land office, was the paperwork finished? Can we start clearing the area and putting down stakes?"

Cort was eager to get off the ground and Victor couldn't blame him. This would be the closest either of them had to a home in years. After the livery was built with lodging for the two of them inside, he'd take the tent and move it back out where the Farnsworths had been before. Having the witch and her brother so close by would keep people from getting too interested in what was going on, yet it was just far enough away that they could gamble there without Winslet getting wise to what they were doing. Winslet couldn't claim they didn't allow anything like it in Blessings, because there was a saloon. Blessings wasn't immune to gamblers.

"He wasn't in, and his *assistant* didn't know anything about the paperwork." Not that he'd asked her. In fact, all thought of the paperwork had fled his thoughts like hounds after a fox as soon as he'd seen her through the window. Her lovely head had been bent ever so slightly over her work, her lip tense... He had to stop thinking about her.

"She didn't know ... or you didn't ask?" Cort tossed the dregs from the bottom of his cup into the grass and leveled him with a steely gaze. Both of them were tired of cooling their heels and using what they had to buy food instead of supplies. Watching the town forge ahead without them was harder than Victor had thought it would be. Now that he was here, and his mother would know where he was after the letter he'd sent before leaving Boston, it suddenly felt like time was of the essence, that if he didn't hurry, *something* would happen.

"She didn't have the papers. They were still on her father's desk." At least, he was pretty sure they were. Farnsworth could be trusted, he'd shown that so far with all their other dealings. Farnsworth had told them the papers would be ready, so they would be. They may have even been ready while he was there, but Cort wouldn't know that.

"I don't see why we need to wait for his paperwork. We've paid, we're already staked on the land. Are they going to take it away now if we show that we want to stay, to live here, to invest here?"

Cort was getting more agitated by the moment and it was time to calm him down before his temper got the better of him. He didn't need Cort going back to the land office and making things more difficult, or scaring Lenora. Bad things happened when Cort got mad.

When a man had cheated Cort out of his winnings in a high stakes card game—winnings that he could've lived on for quite some time—Cort got angry. Then he got even. The cheat woke up the next morning with his prize stallion, a gorgeous Morgan, already in the next state. Cort had taken it, sold it under the owner's name, and left. That was part of the reason Cort was on the run. Coleman Gale, the former owner of the horse, put a price on his head at five times the value of the horse. Cort was to be caught alive and brought back to face a hanging judge. Since Cort couldn't prove he'd been cheated out of more than the horse had been worth, he ran.

Victor went inside the tent and changed into his older suit. He slowly rolled up the sleeves on his newly laundered white shirt to above his elbows. The seamstress, a Mrs. Pati Jones, hadn't wanted to become a laundress, but he'd sweet talked her into washing his two suits. She'd also taken out the sleeves in his shirts and jacket a bit. Though he hadn't had to work much in England, in the last years, he'd had to acquire a taste for manual labor. His arms had grown thicker, chest wider, and hands more callused, but he was also more self-sufficient. Money hadn't bought that, but lack of it had.

Cort stood from his stump with a growl. "I can't believe we'd be expected to wait when everything's been approved."

"No," Mr. Winslet replied from behind Cort. He spun around and the old man waited, scratching his beard and glancing at the area around the tent. "I think you picked a nice area. Away from town, so Blessings won't smell like a horse barn. Your paperwork should be done soon."

Even though it was Cort who'd been rude, Victor needed to make sure Winslet knew they wouldn't start anything without approval. Victor was no fool.

"Cort didn't mean any disrespect."

Winslet laughed. "It'd take a lot more'n that to rile me. I gave the approval, you start when you're good and ready." He met Victor's eyes and the old man narrowed his focus and something passed between them. He hadn't felt that depth of understanding since his own father had cast him away. It widened the hole he didn't realize had been there.

"I know you think you can pull one over on me, Abernathy, but there's more in store for you in Blessings than you think." With that, he turned and left. Victor couldn't help but wonder what he meant, and how he could know what he'd planned when he hadn't even told Cort.

He and Cort took out the tools to start clearing the few trees from their large plot, a plot that would hold a ten stall livery, with a loft for both straw storage and places for he and Cort to bed down. It would also have a large corral. He turned in time to see a vision in a green skirt with a matching velvet shawl tucked into the front, heading right for them, her dark hair was held in place at her nape in a large bun. Though he'd just seen her not a half hour before, he couldn't keep his chest from squeezing tightly. She'd come to him, finally.

He stepped forward and she glanced at him with laughing eyes that dared him to come closer. She veered for Cort and handed him a sheaf of paperwork. Though her voice was all business, even calling her father by his proper name.

"Mr. Farnsworth told me to tell you that everything has been signed and is in order. You may now start building."

Cort tossed the expensive papers into the tent with a grunt. "Thank you, now git. You're a distraction to Victor."

She gasped at Cort's comment and her eyes sought his. Victor was so used to Cort's natural cantankerousness that he had to laugh, and that lit the fire in her eyes even more. Eyes that never stopped captivating him.

"Are you laughing at my expense?"

He smiled and she flushed ever so slightly, her eyes dropped from his and she stared at his bare arms. He almost laughed again. The pretty miss had seen plenty of exposed arms of the crewman at sea and hadn't bothered to give them a second glance, that he'd noticed—and he would've noticed—but *his* arms enticed her eyes?

"Was there something else you needed, love? Cort may have been a bit off-putting, but ever so right. With you standing just there, I will get nothing done."

Her little pink tongue slid over her lips in a quick motion, her glance nervously darting from him back to Cort. It took everything in him not to frame that pretty face with his hands and take a taste of those lips. Would she be smooth like butter, or give him a kick like strong coffee?

"No, nothing. Good day."

She almost curtsied before she remembered the mud and just turned on her heal with her skirts lifted slightly. He took a calming breath as he watched her sway all the way back to her father's office.

"Are you done wool-gathering, so we can work now?" Cort's voice slapped him back into his own mind.

If he didn't convince that woman to be his soon, he'd never get a lick done.

CHAPTER 7

It was wrong to feel as she did, hadn't she sat through Bible lessons for years that told her desiring *anyone* was wrong, much less someone so ... worldly? Lenora sat at her desk facing the window out into the street. Even knowing Victor would be busy building the new livery didn't stop her from glancing up from her work every few minutes to see if he was coming around the law office to see her. He'd hardly missed a chance to visit her for months, yet the afternoon was wearing thin and soon, she'd have to go upstairs and help mother with supper.

Father had agreed to let her work for him under the condition that she would quit if Mother needed her more. Since Mother refused to cook any more meals, that meant Lenora had to be prepared and have luncheon ready before she came down for work, and she had to leave early in order to prepare supper. It was only a matter of time before her father tired of the whole mess and just asked her to stay upstairs, but she prayed he would see her usefulness before that happened.

The sigh escaped before she could stop it, and her father shifted in his desk behind her.

"Something the matter, Lenora?"

She couldn't very well tell him that she'd had a few too many day dreams about a certain rogue Englishman. Her father was far too practical to ever understand the fluttering of her heart, and how she had to throw cold water over it daily. Victor would leave, he'd made that plain, and she wasn't going anywhere, nor would she succumb to the wiles of a rake.

"That little sigh sounded like Matilda used to when I would gaze into her eyes."

Lenora giggled, unable to imagine her parents ever relaxing enough to exchange furtive glances.

"Strange that Mr. Abernathy hasn't been in today, though I know he and Mr. Nelson are working hard to get the livery finished. Many men came to help them so they might finish more quickly. I hope they plan to stick around long enough to return the favors."

Though Victor needed no help in defending his honor—he had never bothered previously—ire built inside her. Her father had no right to condemn Victor, he'd trusted him with the security of his family. That had to account for something.

"I'm sure Mr. Abernathy and his associate will help the other men. They don't seem the sort to take advantage."

"Yes, well, they did manage to get Geoff to lift a finger, so they have my utmost respect for that. I do wonder what they had to do to bribe him. He'd never do it just for the sake of helping someone."

The night her father had introduced Cort and Victor to the family, Geoff had been wound tighter than a grandfather clock. He'd waited until their guests left, then verbally pounced on Father. Mother had left the room, fluttering her fingers over her chest as if it disturbed her greatly. Lenora had never seen Geoff so impassioned, or so offended.

Everything had changed that night, but change wasn't always bad.

"Your brother hasn't been coming home at night. We aren't sure where he's sleeping. Your mother doesn't seem concerned, but I am. I have a reputation to think about."

Lenora almost choked as she tried to stop herself from scoffing at her father. It wasn't as if

Blessings had too many places Geoff could find trouble. He'd probably just stayed with Victor. She'd ask him ... if he ever came in to see her.

"I'd best go up and help Mother." She stood and slid her stool under her tidy desk. It was little more than two saw horses with a few left-over planks from building their home, but it was hers.

"One moment, while I have you alone down here, dear." His face turned a bit crimson and she couldn't imagine why. They had been talking of nothing that would cause embarrassment, unless her father actually *did* know where Geoff was, and hadn't been telling her.

"What is it? Have I done something wrong?" Her heart trembled, and she clutched her skirts to keep her hands still.

"I told you Victor came and spoke to me about you, that I trusted him with my daughter."

Lenora's own face heated again at the memory. How her father could trust the man still surprised her, and further weakened her resolve to stay away. If her father trusted him...

"I don't know how you feel about Mr. Abernathy, but your mother is in no mental position to talk to you about ... men."

Lenora gasped, sure that her face would melt with the heat. Why would her father want to talk to her about that?

"I don't think there is any need to talk at this

moment."

He stood and came to the front of his desk, leaning on it slightly. He'd aged so much since they'd left Boston, with silver streaks adorning the temples of his once black hair.

"I do. Mr. Abernathy may have been a lot of things, and those things put you at risk of losing your heart, dear Lenora. Be wise. If he cares for you, he will wait. Passion can be a wonderful thing, but only if shared between two people who are committed to keeping it that way. I'm afraid Mr. Abernathy knows more about passion than he perhaps ought."

Lenora wasn't sure what she should say, even if she could get words past her constricted throat. Passion? Was *that* what she was feeling toward Victor?

"I don't know what I feel, Father. But knowing his past, I've tried to keep our relationship to nothing more than a friendship." Despite what her heart wanted.

"The Lord made desires, just like everything else. And just like everything in creation, it can be used for the purpose it was intended, or it can be used in sinful ways. We've heard that what Victor did back in England was sinful, but he wants to marry you, Lenora. Then those little sighs and whatever brought them on, aren't wrong."

Her father straightened and turned his back

to her, shuffling papers. If he was as mortified as she, she couldn't blame him. The door swung open just then and Victor came in, a bunch of golden flowers with the most delicate petals she'd ever seen clutched in his fist.

"Victor..." she said it without even thinking in her surprise and his eyes lit up. She had yet to use his given name until that moment; he'd caught her so off-guard.

"Good afternoon." He bowed slightly. "I realized that I would almost be too late to see you today, so I brought you a bit of gold to apologize. It's the only gold Mr. Winslet will let me near." His eyes danced at his joke and he made it to her side in a few short steps.

Her heart still raced after the talk with her father and to have the very man they'd been discussing show up left her unsure of what to say, afraid she might accidentally give away something her father had said in confidence. She accepted the little bouquet and its fragrance gently caressed her nose.

"If you have time this evening, I'd like to show you how far we've gotten on the livery. Would you walk with me, Lenora?"

Her glance flitted from his intensely green eyes to her father, who was still doing his best to pretend he was alone in the room.

"I still have to make supper, it might be quite late after I get everything cleaned up."

She was just itching to go for a walk with him after thinking he'd forgotten her all day.

"Take your time. I'll come back in a few hours to see if you're ready."

She'd been counting the minutes all day, what was another few hours?

Victor quickly ate whatever Cort had thrown together; he couldn't even remember what it was. The sun seemed to set at a doubly slow pace. At this rate, he'd die of old age before he ever got to walk back to Lenora's door.

Her father had granted him permission to call on Lenora, the first time Victor had ever asked such a thing. In the past, he'd never wished to actually *call* on any young woman. Preferring to revel in that which he and a young woman could enjoy in the span of a few minutes or hours and then return to his life, still as unattached as before. A few hours wouldn't be enough of Lenora, a life wouldn't be enough. He needed that job in the mine to provide for her. He'd get all the money back for his parents, inherit it, and give her an unimaginable life in England. He just had to convince her to agree. There were only seven days left of his original three weeks and it seemed rather unlikely that she would agree in that time.

"Are you going to sit gazing off into the stars all night or are you going over there? I'll be up at the tent, minding our business." Cort slapped his hat on and headed for the door. "Don't do anything I wouldn't do."

Victor had to laugh, because Cort wouldn't have called on a woman at all. It was better that he would be out of the way, back at their tent, now hidden in the woods where the Farnsworth tent had been. They'd set up a few small tables and invited men over to gamble away their findings. The quicker Cort could win their money, the faster Victor could leave California.

He checked the time on his pocket watch. It might not have quite been a full two hours, but he couldn't wait a moment longer. Victor rapped on the front door of the Land Office. If no one came, he'd go around to the back. Though most buildings with a residence on top had their own exit down the side of the building, Edward hadn't wanted that. He'd insisted on a main door in the front and the back exit, but the only way to get up to his family was if someone came inside.

As the door swung open, Lenora's dark eyes, set in creamy skin, caught him and wouldn't let go. She was as beautiful as a sunset.

"Father said I might come down and wait for you," she whispered, her soft lips now drawing his attention.

He'd never lacked for words until that moment. She really was going to join him, by choice. Maybe his odds were better than he'd thought.

"If you're ready, it's almost dark and we've got nothing but torches at the livery yet."

Lenora softly closed the door behind her and joined him in the street. Instead of offering her his arm, as he knew every other suitor she'd ever had would've done, he slipped his hand around her tiny waist. She gasped slightly.

"Victor—," she bit her lip.

He pulled her in closer to his hip and gave in to temptation, brushing a swift kiss over her heated forehead. How he wanted to do more, but he wouldn't. He'd not pressure Lenora as he had others. He'd woo her slowly, thoroughly, until she'd have none other than him. Even if it meant he'd lose his own wager.

She clung to the front of his vest and tipped her face up to him. Her soft lips opened slightly.

"I don't want you, Victor," she breathed the words out slowly. The heat in her eyes said otherwise, but he wouldn't tell her that. That would be giving her too much and she might try to hide her tell in the future.

"So, seven days will pass and I won't have you on my arm, headed back to England?"

She stepped away from him and clutched her hands in front of her, her lips drawn into a chilly line.

"I won't follow you to England in seven days or ever. I'm not leaving Blessings." She walked ahead toward the livery, but it held little actual interest for him. She had to come to England, to meet his mother, to be his bride. It had been the only thing he could think about for eight long months.

"I have to return to England, love. You say you don't want to be with me, but if there's any part of you that does, be prepared to leave."

She didn't stop her clipped pace just ahead of him, and though he couldn't find fault in the view, he'd much rather be talking *to* her.

"Lenora. Stop walking away from me."

She whipped around on him, eyes flashing in the waning light. The red of the sunset sent playful streaks of burgundy through her hair.

Her soft voice cut him like a knife to the heart, that she didn't even have to yell to knock him back was just more proof of how thoroughly she had him.

"I am out here with you to see the progress on your building, nothing more. I will never leave Blessings, never. I don't care about your wealth and there is nothing in me that desires it. I've seen wealth. If that was what I wanted, I would stay under my father's roof forever or marry the nearest miner. Some women want more than a handsome face to look at and a pocketful of money." She turned on her heel and strode away from him.

He'd been sure he would need the gold and the social standing to make up for his rather colorful past. A woman as good as Lenora deserved better. In England, his behavior was normal, acceptable, she wouldn't have to worry about the cloud of doubt that would always surround him if he stayed here. Yes, in Blessings, people would always assume he wasn't faithful to her, but it wouldn't matter, because he would be.

He dashed to catch up with her. She'd stopped at the edge of their property, now open after felling the trees. She made no move to speak and it gave him a moment to catch his breath.

"This area in front will be the corral. It will be big enough for many horses. The stable will hold ten, but there will be room at the back, in case we ever need to expand. Mr. Mosier, who drives his ox and cart to get the mail and supplies, has already said that he'd rather pay us to keep his animal than have to try to bring feed back every time he goes. He'll be our first customer. Next time he makes a run to Culloma to get it, Cort will go with him to get us a horse and wagon, so we can get grain and straw whenever we need. Pete, the sheriff, has said that some of his men have horses and nowhere to keep them. It's a start."

He wanted her to understand that he was trying to fit in here in Blessings, even if he wasn't going to stay. The stable was coming along nicely with all the help over the last few days. The structure was up and ready to be painted, they just needed to add doors and then build the fence. He could almost be proud of it, though he'd never planned on having such a business.

A figure appeared around the side of the livery, a tall man with a wide-brimmed hat. He paused for a moment, then headed for Victor and Lenora. Victor didn't know the man and he slid his hand to her hip, despite her sound of protest, and pulled her closer as he rested his other hand on his six. Blessings might be safe according to Winslet, but until he knew the man, he wouldn't let him near Lenora.

The man swiped his hat from his head. "Miss Farnsworth." He reached out and Victor bit back the urge to pull her away from the large smiling man. Lenora placed her hand in his and the man kissed it. Victor squeezed her tighter as anger built up inside him.

Lenora whispered, "Victor, your hurting me." He released her immediately, chastised by her quiet admonition.

"Thank you for your help in finding out the information we needed, Miss Farnsworth."

She smiled at him. "It was no trouble at all,

Mr. Baird. Have you had the opportunity to meet Mr. Abernathy?"

She was going to introduce him? After he'd been such a surly beast?

"No." The man heaved a huge smile and thrust his hand out for Victor. He had a firm handshake and honest eyes. "Benjamin, Benjamin Baird. I help with watching the mines." The man stood back a few paces.

"Victor Abernathy. My business partner Cort and I own the livery."

Benjamin tipped his hat to Lenora and gave her another boyish grin before he strode off into the darkness.

Lenora giggled at Victor's side, and he stopped focusing on the bulky guard, turning his attention instead to the beauty still held against his side.

"You were jealous." Her eyes twinkled as she glanced up at him, her pert lips turned up in a saucy smile.

She slid from his arm, still laughing, and he couldn't speak. He'd never seen such happiness on her face, such openness. He couldn't deny her words and he wouldn't, but what could he do to bring that smile to her face again?

CHAPTER 8

Lenora's giggle would follow him to his bedroll, Victor had to do something to get her off his mind, or he'd never sleep. A woman wouldn't do, but a hand of cards might. He wound his way through town, avoiding any houses and tents with light inside until he reached the confines of the trees. The men were keeping fairly quiet, but he could see the glow of the gambling tent even through the cover of foliage.

Victor ducked inside the tent. Cort, Geoff, and two men he didn't recognize sat around the old door they'd set up as a table. Cort shuffled the worn deck as Victor sat down at the only empty seat. Geoff scowled up at him as the others nodded in quiet welcome.

"Where have you been?" Geoff drummed his fingers on the table, his color rising with the words.

He didn't need to answer to Geoff, or anyone else. He'd lived on his own for too long for such nonsense. Especially since Geoff was little more than a boy. Only the respect he had for Geoff's sister kept him from telling him just where he could go.

"I don't see that it should matter to you where I spend my evening. I came down here as soon as I was finished with what I was doing. Isn't this a place for relaxing?" He gestured around the tent, but it only angered Geoff further. Geoff's face contorted in anger and he slammed his hands down on the table, sending chips flying.

"Keep down your temper in here, young'un, or you can find the door," Cort mumbled.

Geoff raised a bottle from next to his seat and took a long pull, his face was ruddy with drink and movements agitated. He was hankering for a fight and Victor had a mind to give it to him just because *his* blood was up.

"You shouldn't even be here, Abernathy. Blessings wasn't supposed to be for you. You weren't needed. Father should've trusted me, he had no cause to hire you."

It was obvious there was more to his anger

than just the fact that Geoff's father had hired them to keep the family safe. If that were the real issue, he'd be just as angry with Cort, but he'd said nothing to Cort directly.

"And he especially didn't need to hire *two* of you." Geoff growled and knocked back another drink. "Do you think I didn't notice Cort following me around? I started playing cards with you so that I wouldn't feel watched all the time. You think I didn't know that my father hired you to keep an eye on me? That he doesn't trust me? It should've been *me* protecting my family. Instead, he hired some drunk Englishman and a man with no past. He's probably some criminal." Geoff swung the bottle at Cort.

Victor had known Cort long enough that even though he made no visible sign to anyone else in the room, Cort's hackles were up. Geoff would need to calm down and shut his trap soon, or he'd find himself in the river.

"You might be angry about it, Geoff, but it wasn't your father who insisted on Cort, it was me. I don't know why he didn't just hire someone else when I told him that I wouldn't come without Cort, but that's the way I work. It had nothing to do with keeping watch over you."

"My father sat in the cabin of that steamer for eight months with Mother, all while Cort followed me around like I was some sort of untrustworthy thief. And where did that leave you, Abernathy? Trailing after my sister like a bloodhound. Don't think I didn't notice you sniffing. You leave my sister alone. She's too good for the likes of you."

It was true, but he couldn't let it stand. From the moment he'd laid eyes on Lenora, he hadn't succumbed to any of his old ways. And no wandering brother was going to keep him away from her. How much did a man have to give up before his misdeeds were forgotten?

"You haven't cared about your family since they hired us. When was the last time you even slept at home, or talked to your sister? You tell me to stay away? Why don't you act like the brother you want to be and go home? I don't know where this sudden brotherly love came from, but hang it. I've already spoken to your father and he's given his permission to court Lenora as soon as she's willing. I'll visit her every day of the week and twice on Sundays if I get a mind to." Which he did, and young Geoff wouldn't stop him. A whole herd of bulls couldn't stop him.

Geoff jumped to his feet and flipped the table over, scattering the cards and wooden black and red chips all over the ground. The two miners scrabbled for their winnings, but Victor kept his eye on Geoff and he knew Cort did, too.

"Now, you listen, and listen good." Geoff

advanced on him, clenching his fist to his side and pointing a threatening finger to Victor's chest. "You stay away from her or I'll *keep* you away."

Geoff pulled back, but the drink made him slow. Victor nailed him in the mouth and sent him reeling to the floor, a trickle of blood down his lip marred his young face. Pain exploded through Victor's fist and up his arm, but it didn't matter. No one would keep him from Lenora, and certainly not the brother who hadn't cared about her at all for almost a year.

"It's time for you to go home to that family you care so much about, Geoff. Don't come back here until you're willing to calm down. This is a tent for rest, not fights. We aim to keep the Sheriff as far away from this tent as possible, and that won't happen with you blundering around here drunk and hollering."

Geoff wiped the back of his hand across his split lip. "I'll find somewhere else to play before I come back here. You don't belong here," he repeated, "I'll get Winslet to force you out. You won't get my sister."

Geoff whipped open the flap of the tent and stumbled into the night. Victor helped Cort pick up the table, but many of the cards were covered in mud. Playing poker with dirty cards would encourage cheating, so the other two men left and Cort sat shuffling the destroyed deck. If

Geoff went home, would he fill Lenora's ears with more tales about him? She'd heard enough from his own mouth to form a horrible opinion, yet she continued to allow herself to speak to him. That alone gave him hope of redemption in her eyes.

"You think Geoff would really do anything? I've come to think of Blessings as the place where I might finally be able to stop looking over my shoulder." Cort was more relaxed than Victor had seen him in a long time, and it suited the usually guarded man. Victor would end up leaving his friend behind when he returned to England, which was a shame.

Victor refused to let Cort worry. "I think Geoff was drunk and looking for a fight. He's a pup, barely a man, and he's not following in his father's footsteps, so he doesn't know where to place his feet." But no matter his words, Victor still let Geoff's threats sink in. The pup could make things difficult.

Cort snorted. "You didn't exactly follow in your father's footsteps, either. Yet you're not picking fights."

That he wasn't, but he had in other ways. "I didn't need to pick fights, I lost money instead. My father hated gambling, but I was good at it. Whenever he would take me to task for being out late or ask me where money came from, or went ... I would lose on purpose to hurt him. Then, the money was gone, and I had nothing left to lose. Father wouldn't even speak to me. Mother was the one who suggested that I try going to America, land of dreams, to find our fortune once again. I see a lot of myself in Geoff, though, I hate to admit it."

If he could go back and change what he'd done, he wouldn't have ignored his father. The disrespect he'd shown could never be redeemed, since his father had told him to never come back. If he could direct Geoff back to his father, it might even make Mr. Farnsworth trust him more, but what he really wanted was Lenora's trust. That would be more precious than gold.

The lamp cast long shadows over Lenora's small room. Heavy footfalls tromped up the stairwell and she listened to see who it could possibly be at that late hour. Father was in the kitchen, tending to the stove, and Mother was already abed. Only one other person had the key to the doors and he hadn't been home for many days.

Her father's low rumbling voice drifted through the walls.

"Geoff, we need to talk. You've been drinking and haven't come home when you should. Are you a son who lives in this house, or a man who's set out on his own? I need to know. Lenora has taken your rightful place by my side at work, but it's my son who should be taking over the business, not my daughter."

The words hit her like ice down her back. She'd tried so hard to please him, to work and learn, to show him she was worthy of educating. Yet, she wasn't good enough. She'd shown Father that he needed help and he'd turned it all around.

It had been so long since she felt close to Geoff, and now a new wedge would be between them. Geoff's voice chilled her as it drifted through the thin wall, distant, slurred, and tired.

"I'm only here for the night. I'll find somewhere else tomorrow."

"Do you have a job, Geoff? I know you aren't mining. You need money to buy food, find a place to stay."

There had been jobs at the mine, the men were constantly coming and going. Some would tell her there was more gold than a man could ever find in these hills, others were sure it had all been found in the area and they quickly moved on. Though Mr. Winslet wouldn't hire everyone, he would hire Geoff if he asked. Geoff would only need to ask, and he would have everything Victor had wanted from the start. Though it made her angry, she couldn't fault Mr. Winslet, there was wisdom in his decision.

"I'll find something. Don't bother with worrying about me now. I wouldn't want to take Lenora away from her work." She could almost hear the sneer in her brother's voice.

"If you can act as a man, then I have a job for you. Lenora has shown me the necessity for having help in the office, but I want my son to do it. I would pay you a dollar a day to come and assist me."

Lenora gasped at the injustice, first he'd given away her job right under her nose, then offered pay for it, when he'd never offered her a dime. She'd worked, learning everything her father had put before her, yet she would never be good enough in her father's eyes, because she wasn't his son. She'd dreamed of becoming a lawyer, to be a partner in Father's business. Now Geoff, the wanderer, would get that honor.

"You don't want me working for you. You don't trust me. You didn't trust me to watch over the family, and you don't now, either."

"That isn't true." Her father's voice was level, calming, even with her building anger. "I do trust you and I want you to consider taking on the family business, become a lawyer, like me."

"I'm no lawyer." Geoff's words slurred with fierce anger.

"Not yet, but you'll never know if it's something you want to do unless you see what it entails. Go. Sleep in your bed tonight. Get a good night's rest and join me tomorrow morning."

Her whole body was heavy with the weight of the betrayal. For that was just what it was. Her father had used her talents to improve his business, then cast her aside. Perhaps it had been his plan all along. Geoff hadn't shown his face in their home since it was finished. They hadn't known just where he was sleeping and since he was close enough to the age of a man, her father hadn't seen the need to seek him out. Yet the moment he showed up at their door, he was welcomed back with open arms and given *her* dream on a platter. Her heart ached, and she longed for someone to talk to, but who would listen?

Would her father even take her aside and tell her his change of plans, or would he just ignore her? His lack of care left such a deep wound. There would be no helping with transcription or filing, and no excuse to sit by the window and watch for Victor. Without her work, she would have no reason to seek him out, nor would she be able to entertain him. She'd be stuck at home with Mother, who didn't want to see anyone.

Blessings only had a few businesses, a saloon, the mercantile, the land office, the mines, and a seamstress, who was married to the sheriff. The seamstress would be the most likely place for her to find work, though, with so few women living in town, Pati might not have much to keep herself busy, much less another person. The prospects were grim.

Lenora knelt in front of the hard, wooden slab that was her bed and lowered her head. She did not pray aloud for fear of being heard by her father or brother. *Lord, I know you hear my innermost thoughts. I can't just sit here and rot away, helping my Mother who resents me because I want to be here. I came to Blessings to support this town, to be a woman of strength. Help me to find just where I belong, where I fit in. Help me to be strong and not angry about my father's machinations. I do love my brother, and I know he deserves Father's attention and needs his guiding hand. Help my heart to understand that in my loss... Amen.*

Her heart slowed to a normal pace and she crawled off the floor into her uncomfortable bed. Just thinking the words of her simple prayer helped to lessen the hurt. And as the Lord worked on her heart, she trusted it would only get better. Geoff had been hurt, and as a man, didn't know how to deal with it. Father would teach him. Geoff needed Father more than she did. She was an adult, a little older and perhaps wiser.

Yet, even after her prayer, she still had no strong idea of her own path. Before that evening, it had been clear; work with Father and see Victor. It had been many months since she'd gone a full day without seeing Victor. Tomorrow would be a test of her will.

CHAPTER 9

As morning dawned, Lenora pulled herself up from her bed, stiff as the wood slab she slept on. Her feather bed was the one item she missed from Boston and she'd never begrudge anyone who *chose* to sleep on the ground again. For when it was dry, the ground was much softer and more giving than her wooden plank, though at least her plank was off the floor.

The morning light, gently seeping through her thin curtains—made from petticoats that had been ruined on the trip—put the day in order, and she bent her head to thank the Lord for the sun. Finally, after what seemed like forever in the wet and gloomy weather, glorious sun had appeared. It was already warm enough that putting on all her layers was a tedious and daunting task, but there weren't many other options. She wore what women were expected to wear, stockings, drawers, two petticoats, chemise, stays, skirt, and bodice. Dressing never took less than fifteen minutes. Even with the bright rays shining in the window, she couldn't claim the happiness she'd had for the last few weeks, her home felt more like a prison than it had since they'd moved in.

Father waited for her in the kitchen and graced her with a quick kiss on the forehead. Geoff sat at the table, his eyes droopy and mouth slack. It appeared that he could use a few more winks, or coffee stronger than Father was wont to make it.

"Good morning, Brother. Glad to see you." If only it were true. Though she missed Geoff, his appearance had upended her pleasant life.

He shifted his gaze to her for a moment and his lip protruded a bit farther, fuller than she remembered it.

"What happened to your mouth, were you stung by a bee?" She tilted his head to get a better look and he yanked his head away from her grasp, muttering under his breath.

Father approached and pulled out the chair for her. "Your brother was in a bit of a brawl last night, with Mr. Abernathy. I must say, I was a little surprised. I'd thought better of him."

Victor had fought with her brother? She couldn't imagine why, they'd seemed to get along so well, even better than Geoff had with the family. They'd talked the whole way to Blessings like fast friends.

"What could you have possibly said to make him hit you?" She poured a dash of milk in her coffee, it wasn't good to waste it, they didn't have much to spare, but even Father's weak coffee never sat well in her stomach without it.

"What did *I* say? I told him to stay away from you." His eyes narrowed. "And I would think that after he did this to me, that you'd show the respect to your family that we're due and stay away from him, also."

Her heart sank, and she looked to her father for guidance. He'd encouraged her to trust Victor, would he now change his mind? He nodded slightly, in agreement with Geoff and more of her world crumbled.

"I think perhaps we should let Mr. Abernathy make his money and then set his course to mistier shores. I apparently made a hasty decision when it came to my impression of the man."

No, it couldn't be. She'd grown to almost *need* to see him daily. If her father forbade it, she couldn't go against his wishes. She would be stuck in Blessings with no one who understood her. Alone.

"Lenora, I've decided that Geoff will be joining me down in the office. You're welcome to go wherever you need, just please stay away from the tent in the woods, and do give Mr. Abernathy his space until he can either be more civilized or he decides to make this situation right. I'll be letting the sheriff and the men at mine security know of his brawling ways later today."

Brawling? Geoff's lip was barely swollen. It seemed completely unfair. Not to mention, Geoff would've had to seek Victor out, since he'd been with her the evening before.

"Are you perfectly certain it was Victor, I was out on a walk with him until the evening."

Geoff turned dark, angry eyes on her. "Yes, I'm sure. I was in his little gambling tent in the woods, where he plans to make back all the money he's lost, kidnap you, and then run back to merry old England, happy as a lark."

Her father gasped in his shock and Lenora felt her own mouth go slack. Kidnap her? She would never agree to go to England, Victor knew that. But he'd already asked for her hand, why would he feel the need to take her forcibly? Had he really said as much to Geoff? Did her father not realize how close she'd come to accepting? When he pestered her and made her feel like the only woman in the world, it was so difficult to think of reasons to say no.

"In that case," her father's voice lowered to a growl, she'd never heard him sound so, "You will stay *far* away from him and I will certainly bring this to Winslet."

"Father!" She stood, unable to keep quiet any longer. "You all but told me to trust him, encouraged me, even when you knew he wanted to go back to England. You would take Geoff's word without even asking Victor to explain himself? You would besmirch his name?"

Her father took two steps toward her, then stopped. "I've told you what I expect of you, young lady. You *will* obey me."

He descended the stairs, leaving her with Geoff.

She could not hold her tongue. Her stomach clenched and she could hold her words no longer. "You had to meddle, you just *had* to. You haven't cared one bit for any of us, had nothing to say but biting words. I don't believe for one moment what you've said about Victor. And now you've taken away the one person who went out of their way to see me. You came back here because you had nowhere to go, then took everything that mattered to me. Forgive me if I don't welcome you back with open arms."

He slid his chair back and stood, swaying slightly. "I know you don't believe it, but I did it for your own good. He would hurt you, Lenora.

A man like him doesn't change. It's men like him who would turn Blessings into exactly the town that Mr. Winslet doesn't want. That's why he can't have a job. He *does* have a gambling tent, ask him. He *is* planning to go back to England, and he's planning to take you with him, whether you would choose to go or not. He'd steal you if he had to. He isn't the man you think he is, Lenora. Father never should've trusted him."

Her heart had wanted to believe he'd changed. He'd told her of his bad behavior in England, when he'd taunted her with his exploits. He'd told her things that had made her ears burn with embarrassment, but never so much that she would know what she ought not. Though, she had a sneaking suspicion that he would happily teach her should she ever agree to marry him.

But all those other women didn't marry him...

She grabbed her bonnet and rushed down the stairs, avoiding her father as she scrambled out the door. Dash it all, was Geoff right? Was Victor still a drinking, gambling, cad who was only looking to bed her? But if that was all he was looking for, wouldn't he have tried by now? He'd had her alone at the livery just the night before and he'd done nothing. He wouldn't have to take her all the way to England, and if he was as violent as her father thought, he would've just taken her when he desired, yet he hadn't. In fact, his blatant pursuit had slowed and now was almost like he was courting her properly.

She moved further down the street, away from the land office and away from Winslet House, toward the mines. Between them, near the creek, stood a small wooden shack with two windows and an open door. It was the only business on that end of town. The little seamstress shop where Pati, the wife of the sheriff, worked. Though there were very few women in Blessings so far, Pati kept them in dresses and repaired damaged clothing. That little shop was about the only place where she could apply any of the gentler skills she'd learned in Boston. Since Geoff had taken her position, it was unlikely Father would allow her to be a lawyer as she'd hoped—unless Geoff failed, and she refused to hope for that.

Though it was early, she heard soft humming coming from inside the small building. Lenora stood in the doorway and knocked on the jamb. The woman, with short, dark wavy hair and a pleasant smile, looked up from her work and a friendship was forged.

"Morning! What might I do for you?"

Lenora took a deep breath and put on what she hoped was a confident smile. "I'm Lenora Farnsworth, and I'm looking for work."

Birds sang in the trees surrounding the tent and Cort snored softly on his cot, but Victor couldn't sleep. For a man who'd been consumed with pleasures for so many years, he could hardly account for what he felt at that moment, laying on the hard cot that served as his bed. Splinters from the last few days of work throbbed in his hands, and his feet and his back ached. But all he could think about was the look of wonder on Lenora's face when she'd seen his handiwork. A burst of pride like he'd never felt before had rushed straight to his head and hadn't left.

Everything he did seemed to tie to that one woman, and he'd reached the point of realizing that he'd rather never go anywhere again if it wasn't with her. He'd jested with Geoff, telling him he'd planned to steal his sister off into the night if she didn't agree to return with him to England, but he'd rather die than make Lenora unhappy.

If only there was a way to convince her that his heart was true. If he'd never shared the stories of his past with her, she wouldn't have known. But, if he'd been dishonest with her and she *had* followed him back to England, she would've realized his duplicity. Better that he be honest with her and have to overcome what he was, than to have to best a lie.

Cort rolled over and groaned. "What are you doing up before the sun? Don't I work you hard enough?"

Victor could almost laugh. Cort had broken him like a horse the last few days, pushing him farther than he'd ever thought he was capable of. He hadn't realized he could be quite so useful. Now that he'd had a few days to adjust, he was getting used to the rigorous pace of construction, and soon, he'd be used to the dirty job of the stable.

"My wakefulness has nothing to do with how much you expect out of me, friend, though I was beginning to wonder why I insisted you come along on this journey. You've certainly forgotten your place."

It was all in jest. Cort's place was by his side. No man was better, nor could any man be trusted like Cort.

Cort's laugh was more like another groan. "We're brother's, perhaps not in the way of most, but brothers none-the-less."

He couldn't disagree, and he would miss Cort if he did convince the lovely Lenora to travel with him back to England.

"What will you do when I return home? I'd always assumed you would join me, but you plan to stay here, in California. Though, it will work you into the ground."

Cort sat up and rubbed his temples then scrubbed his hands down his face. "California is perfect. No one stays anywhere long enough to notice me. There aren't many people in Blessings, and I can just be who I am."

He'd convince Cort to join him if it was possible, but once Cort had made up his mind, he wouldn't be dragged away from a decision, even by mules.

"Except, you can't. You're *not* Cort Nelson. In England, you wouldn't have to go by another name, you could use your own."

"This is as close as I'll ever come to living free. I'm not going across an ocean and I wish you wouldn't, either. What if Lenora says no? What if she's an American, through and through?"

He hadn't wanted to consider that. Would he choose; his mother, who was relying on him to come home and mend the family, or, Lenora, the lovely bird who'd stolen his heart?

"I don't know. I pray she doesn't force me to make that decision."

"She was born and raised in Boston, where American patriotism came into being. You'd better consider everything before you get too attached to the woman. You think you love her enough to take her home, but does *she* love you enough to go along?"

Cort's question hit him in the gut. Lenora had only recently begun to warm to him, she'd been quite cool to his advances before they'd made landfall. Now, he saw the joy in her eyes when he came upon her. But was that enough? Could he count on her? He was willing to give up every other woman, every dalliance, for Lenora, but would she give up America for him?

"You leave me with a lot to think about."

Until now, his thoughts had been centered around her beauty, but he had to think of her mind and heart, as well. She'd never stay with him if she was unhappy, and he wanted her with him. His desire had grown beyond just that of his body. Her kiss, her touch, her gaze, would be wonderful, but they wouldn't be enough. He'd waited too long for her. Now, he wanted all of her.

"Well, think on it what you will, but while you're at it, it's your turn to make breakfast." Cort rolled back over on his cot and his snores filled the small tent within moments.

After the argument with Geoff the night before, Victor hadn't been able to get Geoff's warning off his mind. Could Geoff turn Mr. Farnsworth against him, destroy all the work he'd done to build trust? It seemed unfathomable. Farnsworth had practically shoved his daughter in Victor's arms, but that hadn't made her want to be there. The road would be much harder if Geoff was successful in changing Mr. Farnsworth's mind. Lenora was a good and respectful daughter and wouldn't want to go against her father's wishes.

Yes, the day held much to think about, but even more work to be done. Victor levered his sore body out of his bed and yanked on his trousers. He'd assumed the gold would flow freely in California, but now that he'd been there for a few weeks, he'd found that the gold—like everything else he'd tried—would be work. However, it would be worth it, and maybe Lenora was just the same. If he worked hard to draw her closer to him, she could be his precious jewel.

CHAPTER 10

Victor put in a day of clearing stumps and working on building the stalls within the livery until his back ached and his hands were bloody. But, they could open their doors soon. After so much help, the men of Blessings were excited about the prospect of having a secure place for their animals. Most of them wanted to have some means to travel, but they hadn't wanted to keep horses or mules outside their small dwellings. Nor had anyone wanted to travel for feed and straw. With the mud all around Blessings, the animals couldn't simply be pastured. He and Cort would have to drive and buy feed for the animals, and the livery would be the perfect place to keep them.

He followed the path he and Cort had worn in the underbrush to their tent and ducked inside to wash his hands and rinse the sweat off his face before he'd go and have his daily visit with Lenora. He'd made her wait until the late afternoon the day before, so now he'd come a little early, just to see the surprise on her lovely face. Not to mention, the more hours he went without seeing her, the surlier he got.

Cort strode in just as Victor was tying his string tie using the small mirror hanging in the corner of their tent as a means to tie it straight. Cort's mouth turned down in disapproval as he stared at Victor's suit.

"Tomorrow we can move into the livery and move this tent out by the other for our evening exploits." Cort sat heavily on his cot. "We were able to spend less than we planned because of so much help from the miners."

Victor nodded and kept his eye on his knot. Cort could stay and repay all the kindness he wanted. As soon as he'd earned enough to return to England, he would. The money wasn't coming in near fast enough for him. California was nice, but it wasn't England, where he could play all day.

"A couple of the men said that Farnsworth had some new help today."

Victor stopped fighting with his tie and turned, now unable to ignore his friend. "New?"

Lenora had said there wasn't so much work that her father really needed her, so why would he add one more?

"His son is now working for him, instead of his daughter." Cort stared at him, Victor could see the need for an argument brewing in Cort's eyes, the tension bunching in his shoulders. Was Cort jealous of his time with Lenora?

"What was wrong with the job Lenora was doing? Why would Farnsworth hire Geoff when he's done nothing but drink and gamble since we arrived?"

And how would he visit Lenora if she wasn't working? He'd have to call on her like any other boring suitor. Lenora deserved more, she deserved excitement and intrigue. He liked that she had to wonder all day when he'd appear, and seeing the surprise on her face daily was something he looked forward to and didn't want to miss.

Cort didn't answer, just shrugged and sat on his cot.

"She isn't in the office at all?" He needed to walk down there and glance in the window, just to be certain.

"No. Like I said, I heard it from two of the men. Men whom I trust." Cort folded his hands but kept his steady gaze on Victor. "So, what are you going to do now?"

Victor sat on his own cot. If he were back

home and Lenora were any other woman, he'd just meet her in secret and convince her to come out in the dead of night, so they could still see each other. But Lenora was too special for such deception, just thinking of anyone doing that to her made his blood boil in a most unpleasant way. Even if that someone was himself.

"I really don't know. Any ideas?"

What Cort lacked in social grace was more than made up for with his intelligence. If Victor couldn't think his way through a problem, Cort might have the answer.

"I think she'll be difficult for her father to peg down. Give her a day, maybe less, and she'll be working somewhere else. It won't take long before word spreads about where she's at. She can't exactly hide."

The man had a point. Lenora was beautiful and almost the only woman available. The men would notice her, and he wouldn't have to look like a fool searching around town. But what about now, this very instant, when his need to see her was enough to fill the sky two times over? For almost a year, he'd hardly gone a day without being in her presence. He'd envisioned what the long-hidden sun would do with her pretty hair, and her glorious blue eyes. Now he'd have to be *patient*. If he'd learned anything, ten years before, when he'd turned twenty, it was that his patience only lasted until the next hand was dealt. Though he wasn't generally a praying man, he prayed that Cort was right and he wouldn't have to wait long.

"I'm heading over to the law office to take a peek and see if she's in there. It may have just been idle talk, perhaps she had to go upstairs to help her mother during the day. Those men might have caught her when she was with her mother."

As weak as the excuse was, it was all he had. He'd told himself for a long time that he went to see her daily to make *her* think of *him*, but somewhere along the way, his own need had grown, and he couldn't stand the thought of laying his head down for the night without setting eyes on her, at least from a distance.

"Do you think that's wise? You and Geoff fought last night. If he *is* working with his father today, where do you think he went when he parted company with us last evening? And just what do you think he told his father? His lip was bloody when he stormed off. He either went to the saloon or straight back to daddy's."

Geoff had been friendly until the night before, but now he had more men who would listen to his whining. Men who might agree with Geoff and fire his angst against his family. He didn't need Victor and Cort for his gambling urges anymore, he could ask any one of the miners. But would Geoff learn, as Victor had, that there was more to life than a hand of cards? Would working for his father force him to make the change, or just hide it better?

"I can't just sit here and wonder where she is." He gripped his knees for a moment, unable to sit still; the need to get out of the tent and be with Lenora more alluring than anything he'd ever experienced before.

"So, head down to the tent a little early. I'm sure someone will be down there soon to share a hand or two. That should take your mind off of her. And who knows, a few days away and you might find you don't miss her as much as you think you do."

Victor had to laugh. "Unlikely. A day without Lenora is like a morning without the sun breaking over the horizon."

"The day still happens, Victor. She's just a woman, and bound to tie you in knots before she works her wiles, then wanders away."

"Emitt, you've been in love, eh?" Testing Cort was too much fun to let the chink in his armor slip.

"Don't ever use that name again," he growled.

"You speak with authority on the fairer sex. Yet, you never seem to look, to sample. That tells me you've been entangled in the past."

"It isn't worth talking about. I'm here and I am who I am. I don't have to ever look another woman in the eye again."

With his own heart so fixed on Lenora, Victor couldn't imagine living a life without desire, passion, adoration, love...

"Maybe you just fell in love with the wrong woman."

Cort slammed his fist down on his knee. "I'm done with this, Victor."

The string tie he'd been so careful with, was now unnecessary if he was only going to the gambling tent.

"What is stopping me from moving into the livery tonight?"

Cort narrowed his eyes with a skeptical glance. "Nothing, except that it's almost evening, we haven't made our meal yet, and there's nothing over there."

Except the new stove, which would make cooking the evening's supper easier.

"Why don't we bring what we can over there, and make do for tonight. I'm ready to sleep under a roof." Which was true, but he'd hoped to have Lenora with him. She'd all but escaped his wager. Perhaps she wasn't as warm to him as he'd thought. It had never taken so long for a woman to succumb, but she would be all the sweeter once she did.

Pati smiled with three pins stuck in her mouth. She took a moment to grab them out then nodded. "Have a seat so I don't have to look up at you." Her lilting English accent took Lenora aback for a moment. It was rare to hear in Boston. Even almost one hundred years after the war for America's independence, Boston was largely colonial.

Lenora came further into the small shack with its plank floor running the whole length of the one room. There were only a handful of women in Blessings, so there would be no need for her to work with Pati, but where else could she go? If Pati didn't hire her, that left the saloon, and her father would never approve of such a job.

Pati turned to face her and gave her a frank once-over. "I don't like doing the laundry. It takes my time away from sewing. You can set your own price, use my basins, but that's all I really have for you to do. Oh, and the occasional embroidery. Some men like their initials on their handkerchiefs so that when they go through the wash they don't get lost. Sometimes I don't have time for that, either."

Lenora had only learned how to do wash on the voyage, and it was much different now that they were on land; probably the least enjoyable chore. After doing the wash, her hands were always red and raw, but if that was the job Pati needed her to do, then she'd do it. The only person in all of Blessings who didn't work was her mother, and she refused to be like her. The reasons for her mother's lack of ambition had changed over the past few weeks.

Mother had gone from distant and angry, to addled. She'd taken to talking to herself. Her eyes would roll back in her head and she'd sway, sometimes sing. Mostly she talked about the Indians, and how terrified she was of them. As far as anyone knew, Mother had never even laid eyes on an Indian, but something had convinced her they were a threat and she wouldn't calm herself, nor could anyone give her words of comfort once she started swaying and groaning in fear. Lenora hadn't told anyone, but her father knew. He'd warned her not to say anything to anyone; not only would they talk about Mother, they might accuse the witch of plying her craft.

Lenora steeled her resolve. "I can do the wash. How often do the miners come in?"

"Whenever they have a spare minute. They'll bring it all in a neat bundle, tied together. You'll need to wash, dry, starch, and iron everything. When you're done, fold it and tie it back together, all nice and tidy. They don't mind paying a pretty penny for it, either. I charged eight dollars a set when I was asked to do it, and don't you charge a cent less."

Eight dollars, that was more than her father

had even *thought* about giving her for a week of work. Lenora took a good long look at her hands, they weren't as smooth and soft as they'd been in Boston, and they never would be again. Soon, they would be red, swollen, working women's hands, but she could say she'd helped the little town in the only way she could. What did soft skin matter, anyway? It wasn't like anyone would take notice of her once Victor left.

"I'll go gather some water and wood to get it heating."

Pati didn't talk much while she worked, and Lenora pressed ahead all day, washing all three sets of clothes that had been waiting, then hung them to dry. While they dried, she'd hoped to do some embroidery, but her hands were burning from the soap, and she couldn't hold a needle.

Pati smiled at her a moment and took a jar of green salve down off the shelf.

"Here, put a bit of this on your hands. The witch none of us are supposed to talk to, gave it to me when she saw my hands after doing the wash. I think it's melted bee's wax, animal fat, and some plants. All I know is it works, so, I don't usually tell anyone where I got it."

Lenora opened the lid and swiped her finger over the oily green lotion. It had no smell, but soothed the burn the moment it covered her hands.

"Good," Pati said, "now, go home and fix

your family luncheon. It will give the salve some time to work."

She did as she was told, especially since it would keep her family from wondering too much about where she was.

When she returned to the seamstress shack—for it did not have a name yet—she rushed through all the other steps until the day was finally spent. She'd managed her first day of work. It wasn't what she wanted to do, a lawyer wouldn't need to do her own wash, but the three neat stacks waiting on the table for their owners made her heart swell with accomplishment. She could see, without a doubt, what her hands had done all that day.

Pati stood and stretched slightly. "I think it's about time we call it a day. The good light is gone, and I can't sit here a moment more. Pete will have done his rounds and will be waiting for me to fill his belly. That man can eat. Will I see you again tomorrow, or did the first day wear you out?"

A small smile played over her gentle face. Pati knew it was hard work and also that Lenora hadn't been used to such chores.

"I'll be back, unless you'd rather not have me."

"Far from it. I think the women of Blessings need to stick together. We are stronger when we do."

Lenora hadn't thought about it, but Pati was right. When she'd worked for her father, it had proved nothing. He'd sent her away the moment her brother showed up. Working for a woman built the business of that woman, and Pati wouldn't replace her.

The skin between Lenora's fingers burned and peeled. She tried to keep from scratching her hands on the way home, since she'd forgotten to ask for more salve. She'd never had to wash so much at one time, and now she'd have her hands in that water every day. Once the miners learned that the seamstress had someone there to do laundry, it would only be a matter of time before she wouldn't be able to keep up. Blessings needed more women.

The seamstress shack wasn't far from the land office, but Lenora took her time, glancing around, strolling more than anything, and trying to convince herself she wasn't hoping to see a handsome scoundrel. She'd been so busy all day that most of her thoughts had been of work, but when she'd been able to stop for precious moments, her mind had, without fail, wandered to the Englishman and how she would manage to see him again.

Her father wouldn't permit it, but she was of age. While in Boston society, she may have needed her father's approval, but not in Blessings. She'd never flaunt her disobedience openly in front of him, but neither could she stay away. What Geoff said had to have been a lie, or at the least, skewed for his own purposes. It wasn't clear to her what those could be as of yet.

When she made it to her door, she could tarry no longer. Victor hadn't found her. They would go an entire day without seeing one another. Unless he came for her as he had the evening before, but if he did, Father would tell him he wasn't welcome to see her anymore. If he did that, Victor might take it to heart and never seek her again.

Lenora whipped around to find where the sun was in the sky and how close to the tree line. She still had a few minutes. Propriety didn't matter when time was of the essence. Lenora gripped her skirt and ran around the building, toward the livery. If Victor was at his tent, she wouldn't have time to find him, because it was in the opposite direction of the livery. As she approached the dark structure, her heart raced. Dare she go inside?

The fence had been erected around the whole front of the livery and it looked exactly like it should, with the marked exception of paint. They wouldn't be able to get that until Mr. Mosier came with the delivery wagon in a few days. Lenora ducked between the rails of the fence and slowly made her way into the livery.

"Victor? Are you here?" she whispered,

afraid to disturb the silence of a place she knew she shouldn't be. A bird screamed at her overhead and she startled.

The stalls were clean and wide, ready for their inhabitants. There was a small stove in the back for when it got chilly, or Victor and Cort needed to cook. Mounds of straw lay at the ready in one corner. All that was needed were horses … and Victor and Cort.

"Did you come by just to see me, love?" his voice rasped just behind her ear, his breath lingering over her neck sent a welcome shock through her.

Lenora turned and Victor waited, alone, holding a crate.

"Victor, you frightened me." And he had, so said the racing of her heart.

"I certainly didn't intend to."

He maneuvered around her and set the crate down by the stove then came back to her. She had the strangest urge to curl up into him and make him tell her the truth, dispel all the lies Geoff had told. But this was Victor, and he was leaving, going far across the ocean and leaving her behind. He was the man she couldn't have because the Lord wouldn't want her to love a rake. Her poor heart was already going to miss him more than she could stand.

"Victor, how long do you plan to stay here in Blessings?"

He lifted his hand, tracing her jaw, seemingly fascinated by it, ignoring her question for a moment. Then he tilted her face up into the waning light. Lenora held her breath, captivated, as if he'd kept her there with so much more than just a mere finger.

"I'll stay as long as I must, and not a moment longer."

"Do you really think there's enough gold in Blessings to replace all that you've lost?" She couldn't force her voice above a whisper, his hand on her face did strange, sweet things to her belly that she would never be able to explain and wouldn't admit to anyone.

"I think I will bring back *more* than I ever lost."

He came in closer, drawing her nearer as he did so. She bit her lip. Would he kiss her? She'd never done such a thing and he'd shared so many private moments with women much more cunning. Would he find her kiss lacking? Did she *want* to be kissed by one so ... experienced?

He drew his thumb along her lip and her breath caught in her lungs. He lowered his face ever closer.

Cort's voice came loud, echoing through the empty building. "I see you invited guests for supper."

CHAPTER 11

So much tension twisted within Victor that he could've punched Cort for interrupting him. He'd almost tasted Lenora. *Finally*. He'd never waited so long for anything in his life and Cort was a thief for stealing the moment.

Lenora backed away from him, suddenly wary when she'd been warm and willing just seconds before. He reached for her hand to keep her close by, but not as close as he'd like, and she gasped, biting her plump lower lip once again. How he wanted to stop her from doing that, and more, how he wanted to nibble it himself.

"Lenora?"

She flinched. What had he done? He hadn't attempted to bring her back to him as he'd wanted to, but there was pain in the lines around her eyes. She tugged on her hand and its roughness registered first shock, then anger within him. His Lenora had been perfect, spotless in his eyes. As he raised her delicate hand up, the red angry flesh tested his will not to seek out and maim whomever or whatever had done such a thing.

She tried again to tug her hand from his grasp. He ignored Cort's grumbling behind them and led Lenora over to a pot on the wall that one of the miners had left behind for anyone working with the roughhewn wood. It was a glass jar with a large cork on top. He popped the lid with one hand, then dipped it in the cool paste within. He wasn't sure what it was made of, but the slick substance helped the men keep their hands from turning to bloody stumps after working with the unforgiving wood.

Lenora's wide eyes searched his as she continued to hold her lip captive between her teeth. Ever so gently, more tentative than he'd ever been with a woman, he coated her lovely hand with the salve. Slowly covering it, taking perhaps more care than was necessary to make sure every inch of skin on her hand was covered with the healing concoction, and enjoying every leisurely stroke of his fingers over her skin.

He reached for her other hand, but his eyes were drawn to her face. What had been pain and perhaps a little fear, was now smoldering. His little Lenora had hidden her feelings for him, but was it enough? Could passion last forever? Now he wanted her to more than desire him, he wanted her to stay with him.

"What did you do today, love?" he whispered, wanting those eyes only on him.

She froze, her soft mouth opened for a moment, still entranced with the workings of his fingers, then blinked as she returned to herself.

"Father didn't need me anymore, so I went to work for Pati."

"The seamstress?" Why would her hands be raw from the seamstress?

"The only thing she needed help with was the washing. It's work, and the miners need it."

She tried again to tug her hand away and now that he was done caring for them, he let her.

"And do you feel accomplished?" He'd worked his own hands to the bone the last few days and it was something to be proud of. Though his family back home wouldn't think so.

She nodded, hiding her smile as she tucked her chin. Victor rubbed the remaining salve on his fingers into his own work-worn hands so that if he was ever able to marry this amazing woman, she would let him put those hands on her.

"I should get back home, it's getting quite late and I still need to make supper." She slid to the side to get around him, just as she'd done on the ship.

"Lenora, love?"

She stopped, and her eyes raked all the way up his body and finally landed on his eyes.

"I *will* finish what we started."

Her eyes went wide for a moment as she understood his full meaning, but she didn't respond.

"You have but three days left on my wager. I'll take you back to England and give you a life like you've never dreamed."

Instead of the joy he'd hoped for, Lenora turned from him.

"I can't. I can't go to England with you and I won't. Father will not let me see you anymore. I'm here ... to say goodbye."

"No. I'll take you whether he wants me to or not. I'll not be kept from you." His anger built faster than he'd expected, clenching something deep within him.

She turned back to face him and this time, it was true fear on her face, unexpected and pure.

"Take me?" She stepped back further.

"I will not be parted from you. I can't. I can't go a day without seeing you. Tell me you don't feel the same. Tell me that's not why you're really here."

He crossed his arms and prayed she felt what he did, like there was a cord between them that was unbreakable and tightening with each passing day.

Lenora dodged around him and headed for the door. Either she was incapable of feeling what he did, or of admitting it. As she dashed from the stable into the night, Cort laughed. The sound grated against Victor's ears.

"You think that's humorous? That she would walk away?" He clenched his fists to keep from starting a fight he couldn't win. Cort would best him physically, but that didn't stop his boiling temper.

"I don't. But I did warn you. She's got you hog-tied, or perhaps in vernacular you can understand a little better, strung tighter than a piano. I told you to be prepared, that she wouldn't want to go with you, and now you've got to decide, mother country, or mother of your children."

Cort turned and walked out of the stable to bring more of the items they would need to make their home in the loft.

The mother of his *children*... He'd never even considered that one day he might want them, but if any woman could make him, it was Lenora. To see her beautiful crystalline eyes looking up at him from the face of a daughter... A fierce need to protect a daughter he hadn't yet made took over him. He'd never let her near someone like him, ever.

And if that was the case, would Mr. Farnsworth ever let a man like Victor near his?

Geoff and her father had been right. Victor would take her, wouldn't be kept from her. While Victor had been right, she couldn't imagine even a day without seeing him—it was the very thing that had tempted her to disobey her father's edict—she wouldn't go to England. Never would she board a ship again, not even for Victor. The sickness, the smell, the heartache; she feared she'd never make it alive.

A heart-stopping terror had clutched her as soon as he'd mouthed the words, *take you.* Since they'd reached Blessings, preventing him from realizing she wanted to be with him had been difficult, because her feelings had grown to where she couldn't stand to be away. However, his idea of the best life she could imagine was most likely vastly different from her own.

She slowed her pace and held her hands out in front of her, hands that had felt Victor's tender ministrations. His soft caress had built a desire to feel his lips on hers even more than when he actually had almost kissed her.

As she entered the land office, Geoff stared at her, taking in her disheveled appearance. The harsh lines of his face leaving a sense of dread over her.

Her father's severe voice interrupted her worry about Geoff. "Lenora, where have you been? Mother will have started supper already. That is one of your responsibilities. If you can't be home on time, then I will not allow you to go about town while we're working."

While her lips said, "Yes Father," her fury built. She'd worked harder all day than he had, sitting at his desk. She'd sweat and rubbed her fingers raw. She clenched her fists in her skirts at her sides to keep from saying what would only make him angry. She wouldn't give in and voice what she felt, she would be the respectful daughter.

As she went up the stairs, the scent of her mother's cooking hit her full in the face. It hadn't taken her more than a week to learn basic cooking skills, out of necessity. Her mother cared little if what she attempted was edible, she rarely ate more than a few bites of anything anymore.

"Lenora!" she snapped, "where have you been? I waited for you to get here. Surely your father wouldn't keep you down there when he knows I need you up here. If he continues to hold you past the time to prepare meals, I will make his life even more difficult. See if I don't. I called down the stairs an hour ago."

If Mother hadn't been attempting to stir

whatever was burned to the bottom of the pot on the stove, she'd have had her hands on her hips. She'd lost so much weight, her dress hung off her. She looked little better than clothed bones.

"It wasn't Father. I was out. I'm sorry." Though she wasn't. Her mother had traveled the same distance, over the same rough seas and the terrifying Isthmus, there would be no going back. She'd held a grudge since the beginning, a useless grudge that now hurt everyone around her.

"Sorry doesn't cook the dinner. Finish this." She slammed the spoon down and strode back to her room.

Her life had been so much easier in Boston, but it wasn't better. She'd been to parties, danced with more men than she could recall. Had been forced by her father to allow certain men to call. Not a single thing about that life had interested her, had stirred her. Laundering clothes for single men wasn't what she'd had in mind when they had set out, but if her father wouldn't support her dreams, and the man who lit her desires wouldn't either, then it was time for her to save for her own fortune.

A future as a lawyer would keep her mind busy, enough that she might not remember Victor when he was in far off England, romancing the beautiful women. At the mere thought of Victor kissing another woman, anger boiled within her—much like whatever her mother had tried to make for supper. The whole meal would taste like ash, but Lenora didn't much care. Her stomach was in knots and her family certainly hadn't helped matters.

Lenora shoved the pot of mystery stew to the back of the stove and set the bowls and spoons on the table. Her father and brother finally tromped up the stairs where they washed up at the basin then came to the table. She clutched the back of her chair, waiting for them to say *something*. No one had wondered where she'd been all that day, or at the state of her mussed hair and clothes. Father would assume that she'd listened to him, and for most of the day, she had. But weren't they even a little curious about where she'd been?

Geoff yanked out his chair and slid into it. "Heard that you were working as a washer woman. If you find any nuggets left in their pockets, you should give them to Father."

Her hands tightened on the chair until the raw red skin was bright white, and her father glanced up at her for a moment before he pulled out his own chair and sat. Neither had gone back to tell Mother it was time to sup.

"I'm sure the miners are more careful with their earnings than that." Lenora could hardly keep the snap from her words. If her brother hadn't come home, she wouldn't have had to change everything.

"I'm going for a walk. I'm not hungry." She grabbed her shawl and rushed for the door before either of them could say anything.

She had no desire to see anyone. Her family was steadily pushing her out and now she feared Victor would load her in a wagon and take off, and while she feared that less than staying with her family, there had to be an option she couldn't see, one that made her heart sing and kept everyone happy. She crept along the path toward the river. There were two tents, all lit, where the Farnsworth camp had been before the land office was built. Men's voices came from within and she changed her course to give it a wide berth. A woman alone didn't need to go anywhere near the tents of men.

The crickets sang in the undergrowth as she made her way to the river. Finally, along the bank, she sat quietly and listened to the trickle and play of the water. A twig snapped behind her and she gasped as the woman in the red cloak appeared at her side. She sat down slowly and stared at her with wide, dark eyes, her creamy skin almost glowing in the moonlight. Her hood was down now, and the cloak thrown behind her shoulders like a cape. She was mysterious, lovely, and frightening.

"Good evening," the woman said in French. "I am Seraphina Beaumont, and you are the first woman other than myself to brave the river alone at night." Her musical voice was soft, and rhythmic, almost alluring. Lenora recalled the story of the Pied Piper.

"Why wouldn't anyone come to the river? It's peaceful." Lenora couldn't ignore the woman. As much as she'd been warned, Seraphina held less danger or mystery than the rest of her life.

"They will tell you that they don't come because of the Miwok, but I know they don't come because they are frightened of me. My brother tells me what they say."

"The Miwok?" No one had mentioned anything about them, and she would've remembered such a strange name.

"The Indian tribe that lives across the river. *Monsieur* Winslet granted the parcel of land across the river to them, to keep them happy. Whether it does or not, I don't know. I have yet to see them."

Lenora clutched her shawl closer about her. Now Seraphina was definitely the lesser to fear. "Is it safe to be sitting here? Do they know we're here?"

Seraphina turned up her lips slightly in a mysterious and distant smile. "That would depend on whom you ask. You are not safe from the judgment of others if they find out you're consorting with the likes of the *witch*." With that, she stood and strode back into the woods.

She held her breath and searched across the river for any movement, her heart throbbed in her chest and she was terrified to move. She blinked slowly and then she saw him. A man stood on the other bank, completely still. He was largely naked, but for a loincloth of animal skin, and paint covered most of him. Her heart stuttered, and she swallowed a scream. If she screamed, everyone would know where she'd been. If she ran, would he follow her?

She closed her eyes and prayed for the answer as she shook like a leaf. When she opened them again, he was gone.

CHAPTER 12

After the scare by the river, Lenora wanted to stay abed and hide, but if she was going to go work with Pati, she had to get up before the sun rose and get both breakfast and the noon meal made. As quietly as possible, Lenora dressed and prepared biscuits, lifted the stew from the night before to the back of the stove, and finally sliced some cheese her family could eat if they found nothing else palatable. She ate her little portion and then covered and left the rest for the others.

The morning was fresh and bright, but it would be sweltering in a few hours, especially over her boiling water. She reminded herself to be thankful. She would earn more than her father had offered. It was a job and it had to be done, so she took a moment to thank the Lord that it was available to her.

Unfortunately for her, the day before, she'd had to refresh her water after each bundle of clothes, because the miners got them so dirty that the water was black when she finished. She'd had to use so much soap to get them clean that her hands might never be the same.

Pati sat outside her little shop in the warmth of the morning sun, her dark hair blew in short wisps about her ears and a soft smile rested on her face as she ironed some fabric. Sounds came from all over the small town and Pati would look up every few moments to watch them. The people of Blessings had all come out once the rain let up to enjoy the end of spring sunshine.

"Good morning, Lenora. Though you'd said you would, I wasn't sure if you'd return."

Lenora pursed her lips for a moment to think about what to say. Pati was the only woman in the town, besides Seraphina, who had taken any interest in her, and she didn't want to stand in the way of a friendship. But she *had* said she would be back. Though Pati also understood how hard the work was to be done.

"I promised you I would, and so I am. I will need to work faster today, though. My father was displeased with the tardiness of my arrival home yesterday. Though, it was partly due to the short walk I took after leaving here. They expected me home before I left yesterday, and I'm concerned my father will not allow me to continue if I don't."

Pati quirked a smile. "Took a short walk? Did you see anything that particularly interested you?" She ignored everything else Lenora had said, that was just work. Pati would let her leave when it was necessary.

Heat raced up Lenora's neck. Victor certainly *was* of interest, but she wasn't quite ready to share Victor yet.

Pati's eyes widened as she took in Lenora's face and gave a slight chuckle. "Oh my, you must have found *something* worth looking at ... or perhaps, someone?"

Lenora took a deep breath and let it go. "I think I'll see to the wash."

Pati's laugh was soft, like the whisper of leaves through the trees, but Lenora couldn't tell her yet. It was difficult enough to admit to herself what she felt.

"You don't have any wash to do. You did it all yesterday and most of it is still waiting for the miners to pick up. I have no new bundles. How are your hands, able to do some embroidery today?"

Her hands were far from fine, but she'd do whatever task she was given.

"Do I need to deliver the laundry to the

men?" Would that be required of her after washing it? It seemed silly to have rushed to get it all done, then let it sit there.

Pati's eyes went wide for a moment and she shook her head. "No, why would I send you to the workman's tent area? Blessings might be the safest boomtown I've seen, but there are some things you just don't do. And one of them is, you don't tempt a man with a steak when he'd be satisfied with a bone. They can come and get their laundry and pay you right here." She pointed decisively in front of her.

Going down to the tent and shanty city near the mines where the miners who hadn't rented plots lived could be dangerous. They seemed harmless, but she didn't know any of them. She'd seen them come into the land office with samples or to inquire about land of their own. Sometimes they wandered down the street to the saloon at the other end of town. Many of them would work for a time in the mines, making what they could in a few short weeks, then leave. Because they were so transient, she feared them; they had no sense of home nor pride in the little town.

Lenora picked up a pair of intricately embroidered drawers from within the basket at Pati's feet. She couldn't imagine who in the town would wear such a garment, but she wasn't about to ask. She examined the pattern that had been started, then threaded a needle from Pati's basket, and they both sat in silence while they worked.

A shadow crossed over Lenora's face and she glanced up as Victor trudged toward them, his gaze was intense and directed right at her. After their last meeting, she wanted to run into the shack to avoid him altogether, but her feet wouldn't budge. Her heart wanted what it couldn't have: Victor.

"Good morning, Mrs. Jones. I've come to order a special handkerchief. Very intricate. Only the best will do, with stitching that will stay fast. I don't want it coming loose, no matter how much it's washed." He turned his green eyes to Lenora with such intensity it stole her breath. "I need the imprint to last a lifetime."

Lenora dropped the drawers back into the basket and held tight to the chair. He wouldn't just take her in the middle of the day, right next to the sheriff's wife, with anyone listening who might hear her scream, would he?

"Good morning, Lenora." He let his English lilt surround her name and Pati gasped.

"I had no idea you were from England. I'd know that accent anywhere."

Lenora didn't want to think about his accent or where he'd rather be. She focused instead on the basket of embroidery between her and Pati and wondered how they would ever get to all of it. If she focused hard enough, she could almost forget the most handsome man in creation stood just a few feet from her.

Victor seemed to press ever closer and the nearer he got, the more her heart raced.

"How are your hands today, love?" he whispered, as Pati set her work aside to look at what Victor had in mind.

"They are working well," she lied. Truthfully, they were sore, and she was thankful they wouldn't have to go near the lye soap for at least one whole day.

"If it's all right, Mrs. Jones, I'd like Miss Farnsworth to do the job."

Pati laughed. "That's fine, all the things in my basket here were just mine, so yours will be paying work. You pay her whatever she thinks is fair."

Victor smiled at Pati and gave her a swift, "Yes ma'am." Then he turned to Lenora, with eyes as penetrating as the summer sun.

"Might we go inside for a moment, so I can show you what I've drawn out?"

Her fingers trembled with the strain of holding onto the chair. He had no business looking at her like that, how could she stay away from him if he didn't stop?

"I think I'd rather stay out in the sun, if you don't mind. I can see better." *And it would be more difficult to scoop me up and run...*

"Lenora, you're shaking..."

He knelt in front of her chair and glanced up at her with his far too handsome green eyes. She would not submit; those eyes and smooth words had tamed too many women.

She swallowed her fear and forced herself to release the chair. "What have you drawn, Mr. Abernathy?"

Confusion flitted over his face for a moment as he slid a small slip of paper from his pocket. On it, he'd written the initials VLA in pretty calligraphy.

"Do you think you can create that for me?"

That wouldn't be a problem, the design was not all that difficult.

"What color would you like it?" she whispered, unable to find her voice.

"I want the V for Victor the same blue as your eyes. Like that of ocean waves on a bright sunny day. The L for Laurence, a perfect rose, like your lips. And the A should be as black, shiny, and soft as the ebony of your hair. Can you do that, Lenora, for me?"

Her heart couldn't keep up with itself and her head swam. Though Pati sat in silence next to her, she could feel her new friend's discomfort.

"I can," Lenora squeaked. "I wouldn't begin to know what to charge for such an item."

She prayed that Pati would give the answer

for her, to stop some of the tension building between them.

Victor handed Pati the sheet and she quoted him what felt like an exorbitant price of three dollars.

He stood and held out his hand to shake on the agreement. It felt like a trap, like he was looking for a reason to touch her again, to enflame all her senses, but she could resist it no more than she could've resisted the urge to seek him out the evening before. She was lost.

As he took her hand in his, he gave it a proper shake, then drew her knuckles to his lips and kissed each one as he stared at her. sending a pleasant tremor up her arm with each one.

"I will check on the progress tomorrow. Good day, ladies." He tipped his hat and left.

"My, it's become rather warm." Pati fanned herself with Victor's drawing and tugged on her high collar.

Lenora had never felt such inner confusion. She desired Victor but wanted him to stay away, to stave off the hurt. Part of her wanted him to whisk her off to England, but a ship was terrifying, even more than a new country, a world away.

"Warm, yes. I think we're in for a hot spell."

Victor felt closer to his old self than he'd been in months, which was both pleasant, and not. The old Victor didn't stand a chance with Lenora or her father. But hadn't he just bested her father and his admonishment? Hadn't he found a way to see Lenora that was perfectly benign in every way? Well, perhaps not completely harmless. He hadn't been able to help getting a little closer to her than was strictly necessary. But with her ready response to him, how could he help it?

Her trembling was disconcerting though, not the reaction he'd expected at all. In all their dealings over the last many months, Lenora had always been strong, a ready and spirited response on her lips that had forced him to parry back. But today, there had been fear in those blue eyes and he wouldn't have that. Lenora need never fear him. He would have to try to hold himself in check better, to regain the comfort. He'd gone too far, and it had frightened her. He would take as much time as needed to woo her properly. Now that he had the livery, if he must he could take all the time in the world. He'd still not heard from his father, and he didn't even know if his return would be welcome.

All that was left to do on the livery was the paint, and they were waiting on Mr. Mosier to deliver the paint and painting supplies. Mr.

Mosier brought goods from the coast, along with the mail for Blessings. Often, when letters came for the miners, they would be handed out to those who were still there. The remaining missives, usually for miners who had moved on, were put in a sack to be returned to San Francisco or Culloma when Mr. Mosier travelled there again.

Victor had yet to hear from his family, but that was not unexpected. He'd run away, like a beaten dog, so he could supposedly learn to value money. Wouldn't they be surprised to learn he valued money even less now. But if they never wrote, asking him of his progress, could he tarry longer, even forever? Every last moment with the lovely Lenora was cause for savoring.

Since the livery was almost finished, yet they couldn't open, he and Cort had decided to take a few days to set up their home in the loft, make sure the right people knew about the tent in the woods and that it was by invitation alone.

They had decided to make their establishment for men only. Everyone had thought that was a lark, because most women didn't drink or gamble, at least not out in public, but it was a rule none the less.

His evenings would change once Lenora was part of his life. He wouldn't be able to stay with Cort at the livery, nor could he continue to help run the gambling tent. But did it matter? If he no longer needed the money of the winnings, could he give it up? There was always the looming mystery of whether his family still needed him, or even wanted him. If they didn't, was he free?

Would Lenora approve of his tent activities? And what would she do while he was away running the gambling business? She couldn't join him there, not that she would want to, but how would she spend an evening without him? Would it bore her to be alone? He didn't know. They had spent so much time seeking out each other's company that he didn't know what she did when he wasn't with her. Even after a week on the trail with her, she'd done little more than sit there and listen. When he visited her the next day to check on the progress of his handkerchief, he'd have to find out. He had to know. It was just another mystery about his Lenora to solve.

CHAPTER 13

It had taken her the entire day, but she'd finished Victor's kerchief. It now sat, pressed and ready, on the table with the finished laundry. Pati hemmed a skirt and hummed a tune as she worked, and Lenora ported the water to heat for her one and only load of wash that day.

Victor would stop by, soon. He had to. If she spent the whole day looking over her shoulder, waiting for him, it would take her all day to complete the one set of clothes. She'd taken leave of her senses for sure. But the question remained, if he really wanted to nab her and take her to England ... why hadn't he? Was his lack of gold the only thing keeping her in Blessings? If that was the case, the mine could never hire him, nor could her father ever rent him a plot.

He wouldn't be able to nab her when she wasn't at work, as he would have to get by both her father and Geoff to get to her. That meant she had to stay watchful while at work. But if he *did* try, would she fight it? Blessings was home, but was it home because she wanted to be there, or was it home because she'd never known it without Victor? With her family so torn, her small group of acquaintances in Millie, Pati, and Victor, were all that kept her there, and Victor took the lion's share.

She prepared all her tools as the water set to boiling. She slowly put each piece from the laundry bundle into the pot, using a large wooden paddle to stir all of the clothes around. That would help get some of the mud off the hems of the trousers and thick grime from the sleeves. The soaking was hot and difficult, and the stirring was strenuous work, but much better than the next step, which was where she used the lye and scrubbed all the stains out.

After an hour of scrubbing, the miner's shirt and drawers were washed and drying on the line as Lenora worked to get the trousers spotless. Sweat trickled down her neck when Pati called, "Good day, Mr. Abernathy. Your handkerchief is waiting inside."

Startled, Lenora's gaze shot up, landing on

Victor in a pair of snug trousers that accentuated the lean muscles of his legs, his linen shirt had come untucked with the work of the day, and he'd unbuttoned the top few buttons. Lord, why did he have to be so handsome when she felt so humbled? Lenora's hands were sore and raw once again, and Victor was the last person she wanted to see when she was holding back tears. But if she stopped what she was doing, she might never convince herself to finish the job.

Victor stood and talked to Pati for a moment, but she couldn't hear what they said. He examined the handkerchief, and pride swelled in her chest as he ran his thumb over the embroidered letters. He nodded to Pati then glanced over to her. After being caught staring, she set back to doing her work, dropping the soap in the water.

"Good afternoon, love. Splendid work for me, thank you." He held out the money and she stood to accept it, running her dripping hands down her apron first. His fingertips brushed her palm as he slipped the coins to her. She counted it quickly, as it felt too heavy to be correct.

"Wait, Victor... This is double the amount. I can't take this." She tried to hand it back to him, but he gently closed her stiff fingers around the coins.

"Yes, I need you to make another one, to keep you out of that horrid water. You don't have to have it finished by tomorrow, though, I may stop by to check how you're coming on. With the stitching, of course." He smiled one of his devilishly handsome grins that made her stomach do an elated flip.

"Of course. You aren't allowed to come see me." She played along with his game, understanding that this was how he planned to continue visiting her. Just how many kerchiefs did one man need, though? She would have to slow down in her embroidery or risk taking all his money.

"And when you have a drawer full of these, worth more per ounce than gold, what will you do then?"

His smile deepened, and his green eyes popped with mirth. "I'll think of something else. Maybe I'll offer you a job at the livery. At least if I'm going to pay so heartily, I should be able to see you all day. I don't enjoy cooking. Maybe I could hire you to cook meals for Cort and I. Then again, if I had you about all day, I might find it difficult to let you go."

The more time she spent with him, the less she wanted him to leave, but she dared not even hope for that.

He leaned in closer, his breath fanning the hair by her ear. "I want you to make an honest man of me, Lenora. No one can do it, but you. I've tired of thinking of lesser women, chasing them about as if they matter. No one matters but you, love. I won't make you answer me today, but soon. I'm not a man who likes to wait."

She was struck dumb, unable to speak as he turned to leave her. Marriage, to Victor. He'd teased, even hinted, but never had he come right out and asked her. Her voice wavered, and she would've screamed 'a thousand yeses' if not for the lump in her throat. She swallowed and gave herself a minute to catch her breath ... and her thoughts.

"Victor, wait!" she called for him once again.

He paused, that smile still in place.

"I need you to be honest with me."

He cast a glance to Pati and when she continued in her work without giving them a moment's glance, he came back to Lenora. He stood too close, as he always did, the scent of freshly cut wood clung to him. She told herself to breathe.

"Ask me anything. Except to go away. I won't do that."

A breathy laugh escaped her. Victor made her think and feel like a woman; desire, expectancy, dare she admit, even love? She couldn't say, she'd never experienced them before. "You were ... very ... *frank* about what you wanted from me on the ship."

She felt a wave of heat rush up her cheeks, remembering his insinuation about his bunk being the most comfortable berth available. Not only that, when they'd had to sleep in the wagon, he'd said it was pleasurable sleeping next to her.

"I don't deny it."

She closed her eyes, praying for the exact words as they seemed to slip away from her. Just his presence stole her very reason.

"Are you saying that *isn't* your aim anymore?" She forced her eyes to open and stare into the green depths of his. Intense jade with golden sparks took every other thought away.

Lenora closed her eyes for a moment to break his power over her. She wouldn't be just a man's liaison. If he were to have her, it would be only her, and he would swear, before God, to be faithful.

"I intend to go about it in the most honest way possible." He paused, and she wanted him to touch her, even her hand. Her whole body was alive with just the sound of his voice next to her ear.

"But my desire *has not changed.*"

She gasped. He was always so direct, so indiscreet. "What exactly are you asking for, Victor?" She had to know, in plain terms. If he wanted to marry her, she'd say yes because she couldn't imagine having to continue avoiding him when she wanted the opposite. But then she would have to follow him. If he chose England, would she be able to be stronger than she thought? Could she do that for him?

He lifted her sore and throbbing hand to his lips and kissed the soft flesh at the base of her thumb, sending a pulse racing straight to her heart.

"I'm saying, you'd better let these heal, before you give them to me."

Her breath stuck fast in her lungs as he walked away.

He wanted her hand in marriage.

As she glanced down to her chaffed and swollen fingers, she wanted to cry. The one man that wanted her and whom she couldn't imagine living without, was the one man her father would never agree to now, and he was the only lawyer in town to perform marriages.

Pati closed her shop shortly after Lenora finished her washing, and Lenora made her way back to the land office. She'd never really thought of it as home. Since they'd left Boston, nowhere could be called home. She walked into the office and Father was alone, sitting at his desk.

"Where's Geoff?" She removed her bonnet, flinching as the string rubbed across her hands.

"He's gone. He tired of working at a desk, he tired of Mother and her needs, he tired of my rules, and of Blessings. He packed up his bag, took his pay, and has left for San Francisco."

She wished she could dredge up some

sadness, but her brother had left the family months before, this had only been a short visit, to say goodbye. She could have told Father that Geoff wasn't ready, that he needed to grow up first, but he wouldn't have believed her. Now, he would need her to return to help him. Despite her respect for him, she wouldn't do it unless he heard the truth about Victor, or at least listened to her.

"Will you need me tomorrow?" She waited by the stairs. Father was being very quiet. Geoff had only been living with them a few days, not enough time for Father to form any opinion on Geoff's future, not after her brother had been hostile for so long.

"I'm not sure. Something is wrong with your mother. She's not well."

Lenora sighed. Her mother had been unwell for a long time, and as much as she hated seeing it, her mother wasn't going to get any better in Blessings.

"I don't see anything that I can do for her. She doesn't want me near her. She refuses to associate with anyone who wants to be in California. Geoff should have taken her with him."

"Lord knows, I tried," he whispered.

She had only said it in jest. The idea of her mother living away from Father couldn't be borne, yet, was she *really* living? She barely ate, sat in her room terrified, refusing to even go outside, relegating herself to using a chamber pot.

"You asked him to take her along?"

"Yes. But he was not ready to take on the responsibility. I'm not so sure he can even handle himself. But he is eighteen, and this is California."

How many times had she heard that sentiment since they'd come, in passing. It was the reason for everything, because anything was a little closer to possible in California. But father was right, Geoff was nowhere near ready to handle Mother as he wasn't even acting like someone who could take care of their own needs.

"I will pray he finds who he is and that he will come home once he does."

Her father nodded and heaved a sigh. "I suppose you would like your job back?"

She stood straighter, because she couldn't show weakness. "Only if you're willing to admit that Geoff was wrong about Victor."

He closed his eyes and his face crumpled. "I'm going to lose you, too, aren't I?"

"Eventually, yes. I believe him to be the man you thought he was before Geoff's interference. Will you give him another chance, please? All those months aboard the ship, you had him watching me, following me. On the way here, and even once we got here, you had him stay close. If he were going to take me ... he'd have done so already, Father. Don't you see?"

He avoided her question. "You've been working for Pati, will she manage if you come back here?"

"I should check with her first. It wouldn't be fair to just leave."

"You go to her tomorrow, finish what you need to, and ask her if you can come back here. I suppose now that you've had a taste of earning money, I'll have to pay you."

Lenora clenched her swollen fists in her skirts. She'd earned more than her father would ever suspect, but it had cost her. "Yes Father. I think a good wage will help you keep good employees."

She didn't need to point out that she wouldn't even have left if he hadn't hired her brother to replace her.

"I'll go talk to Victor later. Why don't you go up and start on supper before your mother gets to thinking she has to do it?"

Lenora smiled and rushed up the stairs, gasping as her mother climbed out the window on the landing above her.

Cort wasn't a man to run, so watching as he ducked under the fence and ran toward the livery, set Victor's mind to whirling like a top. Cort's eyes were wide and frantic, more things Victor had never seen, and now he was on edge.

Cort ran straight at Victor and collapsed against the side of the stall, panting, where Victor sat.

"Get ... to ... Lenora," he breathed, holding his chest. "Her mother's ... on the roof."

Victor jumped to his feet and took off out the front of the livery and down the block toward the land office. A large crowd—by Blessings standards—stood around the building. Atherton Winslet stood, legs apart, completely in command, calling to men to get blankets in case she fell, to try to catch her. His old hazel eyes never left Mrs. Farnsworth. By the look in her gaze, she didn't want to be caught. Sheriff Jones, whose hat usually covered most of his face, wasn't hiding today. He stood next to Atherton, focused and worried. He wasn't fooled, either. He was doing his best to get people to move on. But the people of Blessings, those who really wanted to be there, were invested in making it a good place to live, and helping out anyone who needed it.

Victor scoured the crowd for the lovely curly head of his beloved when a collective gasp had his eyes back on the ledge and then he couldn't tear them away. Lenora had climbed out the window and was now clinging to the side of the building, trying to get to her mother.

Dear Lord, No!

She couldn't fall. He hadn't prayed in years. The Lord didn't need any requests from his soiled lips, but he couldn't help himself. Victor couldn't breathe as Lenora clutched her skirts and climbed, just as her mother had, to the roof.

He shoved his way up through the crowd and to Sheriff Jones.

"How can we get all these people out of here? They're going to distract Lenora or her mother, and one of them will fall."

Pete's steely dark eyes bore into Victor for a moment. "If these people can help, then I won't send them away. I didn't sign on for this kind of job. Thieves and the like, those are easy. Women … never know what they'll do."

That was true to a point, though many of the women of his past had been easily controlled. Then he'd met Lenora and learned that he didn't want to control her, but to parry back and forth like experts at swordplay. It was delicious. But that would all come to an end if Lenora slipped. Where were her father and brother?

Victor came around to the front and ducked into the land office. All the town was so busy watching, they hadn't bothered to come inside. Mr. Farnsworth sat at his desk as if nothing were going on twenty feet above his head.

"Edward, your wife and your daughter are

on the roof. Don't you think you should go upstairs and try to help get them down?"

He stared at Victor for a moment, and then squinted. "On the roof?"

Victor ignored his confusion and ran for the stairs.

"Wait, you can't just go up there!" he yelled, but Victor wasn't listening.

He took the stairs two at a time until he reached the landing and the open window. He stuck his body out and sat on the sill, leaning back to see as much as he could.

"Lenora," he called up to her. She leaned over the edge, fear turning her face pale as a sheet.

"Victor? What are you doing there?"

"Never mind that, just get down from there. Someone will go up and help your mother, but it need not be you. Can you slip back down to me? I'll catch you."

She shook her head. "No, I'm not leaving her. She's very frightened. She thinks someone came in her room today, and she tried to get away. I can't get her to come."

"Lenora, listen to reason, please!" Cold fear ran down his spine.

She closed her beautiful blue eyes for just a moment. "I'm sorry, Victor." Then her head disappeared as she leaned back onto the roof.

He wanted to curse. There wasn't a whole lot

of room up there. They would need a tall ladder or even a length of tree to lean against the building so the women could climb down. Victor ducked back into the building and Edward stood there staring at him.

"My wife climbed out on the roof?"

The poor man was out of his senses. "It would seem so, and your daughter followed her to keep her from doing anything rash. Though I fear, if your wife should decide to jump, she would probably take poor Lenora with her."

"This has to stop. This irrational fear is putting everyone in danger. The whole town will be talking about this now."

Victor grabbed his arm roughly, unable to believe he could be so unfeeling, even if he weren't thinking clearly. "Surely you care more about the fact that they could die, then that the town will talk! What is she so frightened of? Lenora said she was worried someone had been in her room."

Edward sighed and turned to go down the stairs and Victor followed.

"She has been frightened of the Indians from the very first time you mentioned them. She saw how you followed Lenora around and that convinced her there was something terrible behind every tree. It also convinced her that I cared very little for her, since I didn't hire someone to watch *her* every move. No one has ever even seen any of the Indians as far as I know, and *she* certainly hasn't, since she's been upstairs since we built it."

"Well, something happened, and it's put them both in danger. I'll go see if I can get the ladder from the loft in the livery. It's tall."

"Victor. Thank you. Maybe I was wrong about you."

No, he hadn't been, in so many ways. Victor wasn't the good man that Lenora deserved, but he was trying. He'd win her heart ... if her impetuousness and stubbornness didn't kill her first.

CHAPTER 14

The roof pitch didn't allow Lenora much movement, and her boots didn't grip the slippery flat wood shingles. She should be scared, terrified, but all she could think about was finding a way to get her mother off the roof. Lenora inched closer to her mother, and her mother wrapped an arm around her shoulders and patted her arm in a protective embrace that felt strangely cold and false.

For as scared as Mother had been since they'd arrived, she appeared calmer than she'd been in months. "That's fine, dear. Isn't it lovely up here? Do you feel the cool breeze? I should have come up here sooner." Her eyes were far away, and her face glowed with peace.

"Mother, we shouldn't be up here. Let's find a way to get down." The drop had to be close to thirty feet, and Lenora was fairly certain that she wouldn't survive it unscathed if she fell. Or if her mother suddenly turned against her and pushed her off.

"Nonsense, dear. The Indians have broken into our house. It isn't safe in there, but I'm perfectly safe up here. They won't climb, you see. They only hide behind trees and behind my door. We are fine on this ledge as long as we stay still. They are very good at sitting still. When they do, you can hardly see them. Just sit and enjoy the breeze."

A cold chill ran through her as she recalled the Miwok man in the forest across the river. She knew her mother was right, but how had she known that unless she *had* seen them? Was her mother more sane than they had thought?

"Mother, they couldn't have come in the house. They would've had to walk right by Father downstairs, and they would've had to make it across the river, past the seamstress shop, across the street, and up the stairs." If she spoke reason, perhaps her mother would give up her perch and come down. Though mother's words seemed to have a grain of truth, it just wasn't possible.

Mother tensed slightly but did not move. "Your father let them walk right by. He knows how I fear them and he thinks it's silly. He is punishing me for disagreeing about coming to Blessings."

Lenora could not figure what her mother would've seen that had made her think anyone had been in the house, but it could have been anything, including her own mind.

"The only one who came up the stairs was Geoff, Mother. He is gone. He left for San Francisco this afternoon."

Matilda shook her head and swayed. "He will have a tough time of it. He looks more like me than you do. Darker, like me. You only got the curly hair; you're fair of face, like your father."

Her mother had always flatly denied having any African blood in her veins. Though her skin was a little darker and her hair curly, Lenora had never believed it, because of her mother's denial. But did that mean she'd lied all this time, or that she was merely worried about her son?

"I should think he would be fine. He's been living in his skin until now."

Adding more worry onto her mother's shoulders was not going to convince her to come down, especially when she seemed to get more comfortable the longer she stayed.

"I never let you know my parents, nor did I ever admit who my parents were while we were in Boston, because there is still so much shame in it. Everyone was right, you know. There's always a kernel of truth in gossip. My mother was a proud mulatto woman, who caught the attention of a man who owned a large parcel of land in Missouri. They married, but avoided associating with many people. You also have two uncles. They both look like our father. I was neither dark like my mother nor white like my father, but I did acquire my mother's hair."

Lenora had similar hair, though it was a different texture than her mother's. Lenora's was very soft, thicker than any other woman she knew, and so curly it took an hour after a bath to get a brush through it.

"Why didn't you tell us? It didn't matter, Mother. We wouldn't have treated you any differently."

Matilda sighed and smiled. Lenora wanted to smile back, but Mother was so very sad and lonely. Lenora couldn't muster it.

"*You* wouldn't have, but as long and fiercely as I denied it, others had to assume it was at least possible that I wasn't what they claimed. So, because of my lie, you were treated as the other young women your age."

Her eyes hardened for a moment and she squeezed Lenora's arm painfully.

"Didn't you see them at the docks, auctioning the women from the orient for the brothels? It might not have been in front of a huge crowd, but they didn't try to hide it, either. A man is still measured by his skin, and a woman ... harsher still. They were no darker than me."

Her words were painfully true. Lenora had seen the women; so thin they looked more bone than body, led off the ships and right to a makeshift stage. Father had led his family away quickly, but the sight had been burned in her memory.

"Does Father know that you have brothers? Where are they?"

"No. When I die, that knowledge goes with me. Though, I think your father probably remembers the little town where he found me. That's where my parents still live. I have written to my brothers over the years, but they have no interest in you or Geoff. I am dead to them."

She'd always known her grandparents lived somewhere within an hour of Boston, but she'd been told they didn't *want* to see her. Would they seek her out, come to Blessings, be a part of their lives? Just because her uncles held some grudge did not mean her grandparents did.

"I had a dream last night, Lenora. A dream that I could just fly away if the Indians came to get me. I stuck my head out that window and I felt free for the first time in years. I've had to pretend I was someone I'm not for so long. Then, the Indian started chasing me when we got to

California. I was not made for this land, Lenora. I need to go home."

Her mother had climbed out the window to fly. *No!* She'd thought her mother selfish for her fears all this time, but she couldn't lose her mother. Not like this. Lenora clutched her arm and held it tightly. Men couldn't fly, but they could fall. From where they sat, Lenora could hear the voices of the people below her, yelling, but she couldn't make out what. She couldn't see them from where her mother had them perched by a gable and she wouldn't lean over as she had when Victor had called to her.

"Surely you know that you can't fly. This roof provides no freedom for you. Not really. Let's go back in. Perhaps Father can take you to see a doctor in Culloma. That would be nice wouldn't it?" Lenora gently rubbed her mother's arm, and prayed that someone would come soon to help her.

"Please, let's get one of the nice men to bring a ladder and we can climb down. I'll make some supper and we can just sit at the table."

A wooden ladder bounced against the roof, then creaked with each step as someone climbed up. Mother grabbed hold of Lenora's arm and sucked in a deep breath.

"He's coming to get me again. We've got to go. Lenora, save yourself!"

Mother yanked her to her feet and Lenora

slipped on the sharp pitch. Lenora screamed and tried to free herself from her mother's grasp without slipping off the edge of the roof, but her feet wouldn't find purchase on the slippery wood shingles. Victor appeared at her side and her mother screamed, "Don't let him get me!"

Mother's arms flailed for a few moments and Lenora tried to break free of Victor's grasp to grab hold of her, but Mother fell backward off the roof. Victor tucked her head into his chest, but even the beating of his heart wasn't loud enough to drown out the thud as her mother hit the ground.

The narrow ledge at the edge of the roof and his own arms around her waist were all that kept Lenora from joining her mother in a heap on the ground. When he thought about what could've happened … he had to stop himself from shaking. The roof had been built as expected of a standard two-story house. But instead of the roof having overhanging eaves, they'd built it with flat channels along the edges to direct the rain water away from the house. Mr. Farnsworth had wanted to make sure a building could be built right next to his own.

Victor carefully slid her along the flat channel to the ladder then helped Lenora find her footing. He held the ladder steady as she slowly climbed down. Pati waited at the bottom and led her off as soon as her feet touched the ground. He'd wanted to see Lenora, hold her, make sure she wouldn't fall apart. She'd been shaking as he'd held her. Never had he done anything in his life that mattered until that moment. He'd never stepped into a situation and helped anyone.

He swung onto the ladder and came down.

Mr. Farnsworth met him at the bottom and grasped his shoulder tightly.

"You heard her before she fell, Jones. She said *he* was coming to get her."

He shook Victor and shoved him at the sheriff. "How often did you sneak into my home to scare my wife? You always managed to come to the office when I wasn't there. I thought you came just to see Lenora, you must have found a way to watch and go in to sew terror and discord in my home. Pete, I want him charged with murder."

"Murder?" Pete narrowed his eyes and cocked his head. "You saw as well as I did that he didn't go anywhere near her. Even if he didn't follow orders." The sheriff glared at him.

Mr. Farnsworth's face flushed with deep color. "My wife is dead, and I'll make sure that justice is served." His hand shook as he pointed at Victor.

He hadn't done anything, he'd only grabbed hold of Lenora because in her fright, Mrs. Farnsworth would've taken Lenora over the edge, too. He couldn't let that happen. He'd gone up there to help both women down, but Mrs. Farnsworth's eyes had been wide, frightened. But not as frightened as Lenora. She'd been terrified. Mrs. Farnsworth had known just what the decision to jump meant, and she'd done it anyway.

Pete leaned in close. "The man is bereaved and distraught. Let's go over to the mine office and talk about how to handle this."

Victor could only nod. He didn't care what Mr. Farnsworth thought of him, only his daughter. Would she hold it against him, too? Did she, even now, think that his interference had caused Mrs. Farnsworth's death?

They got away from the dispersing crowd of people, though there was a small group helping Mr. Farnsworth. They would probably take poor Mrs. Farnsworth to Blessings Chapel. Blessings didn't have any other place to keep the dead before burial.

Pete led Victor toward the mines and the small building that had once been mine security. Now it was used to house prisoners, whenever the small town was unlucky enough to have them. Victor was empty inside. He'd wanted to protect Lenora, help her. Instead, he'd frightened her mother and then hadn't been able to follow her when Pati took her. Even now he had no idea where she had been taken.

"Your wife will take good care of Lenora?" He couldn't stop from casting a quick glance back at the seamstress shack, not far from the small building where they were headed.

Pete frowned and kept his pace to the office. He'd already said more in one day than Victor had heard him speak in the weeks since they'd arrived. He shoved the door open and Victor followed, collapsing in the chair opposite of Pete's desk.

Pete rested his elbows on the scarred wood top and stared at Victor for a moment, rubbing a long, pale scar just over his left ear...or what was left of his left ear. Victor had heard the stories of the quiet, brooding mine security officer turned sheriff who'd been the victim of an ambush in the Mexican War. Victor could only respect a man who continued to serve after such devastation.

"You want to tell me why you climbed that ladder when I told you to keep your feet planted on the ground? I don't talk to myself, Abernathy."

He couldn't have stopped himself if he'd wanted to. Lenora was up there and could've fallen. He hadn't been able to hear much of anything beyond the rushing in his ears. The horrible noise of Mrs. Farnsworth's fall could have easily been his beloved, and though he'd known, up until now, that he wanted Lenora completely, he hadn't realized how attached he was. All he could think about was that he'd never held her, never told her that she'd overtaken his heart. And even though it wasn't worth anything, he'd gladly give her everything in him, if she'd take it. Somehow, Lenora could make him worth something; just being with her would make him a better man.

"I couldn't stand to see Lenora up there. I had to do something. What if she'd have fallen? A woman up there, walking on that narrow ledge in heeled boots..." Words tumbled from his lips to avoid saying what he hoped was obvious to the sheriff, because he couldn't admit it to the sheriff first, not when Lenora had yet to hear it from him.

Pete took a minute to think on what he'd said, he leaned back in his chair, his eyes dark and penetrating. "What did Mrs. Farnsworth mean when she said, 'he's coming to get me again?' Have you ever been in the Farnsworth home? Mr. Farnsworth leveled a pretty serious accusation against you, and I can't just ignore it."

Victor ran his hand through his hair, now wishing he'd found someone to trim it. It had been another thing, like so many others in

California, that seemed unnecessary now that he was here.

"I've only ever been in their house when I was helping to build it. I don't know who or what Mrs. Farnsworth saw, but it wasn't me."

He'd swear on a Bible if he had to. If he'd ever had a mind to visit the upstairs of the land office, it would be to visit Lenora, not her mother. But then, he hadn't seen Mrs. Farnsworth at all since the family had moved in.

He scratched his chin and met Pete's obsidian eyes. "Don't you find it a bit odd that Mrs. Farnsworth never came outside? I don't mean to be indelicate, it's obviously a serious situation, but she doesn't shop, doesn't come out to get water, doesn't even come out to use the privy. Most of the town only knew she was Edward's wife because she climbed out of his window. Why would a woman stay holed up in her room for weeks?"

Pete was a man of few words and he seemed to be almost chewing on his thoughts, letting the facts sift through his head before he said anything. Maybe he knew more about Mrs. Farnsworth than he was letting on, but Victor doubted it. The only ones who could answer those questions would be too bereaved to give them.

Victor cleared his throat and continued. "Also, there *was* someone who could get by the front door and Mr. Farnsworth easily, someone who didn't much like his mother or father. And, he's now gone. Geoff."

Pete shook his head. "I don't think Geoff is any kind of model citizen, but I don't think he'd scare his own mother to death. I don't know why Mrs. Farnsworth never came out, maybe she didn't like the rain. It only just stopped. We can't speculate what went on in that woman's head."

While it was true, Mrs. Farnsworth hadn't liked the weather, there was more to it than that, and now that he was being accused of killing her, he wanted to know what that was. She hadn't come out much on the ship, but the farther they'd gotten from San Francisco, the more eccentric Mrs. Farnsworth had become.

"Mind if I go talk to Lenora? I'd bet she could tell us everything we'd like to know."

"I *would* mind." Pete nodded and leaned back in his chair. "My wife is with her right now, and Pati'll know just what Miss Farnsworth needs. And that *isn't* to be asked a bunch of questions by the man who stands accused of killing her mother. I think you should wait here until everyone has cleared out of main street and then quietly make your way back to the livery. Stay up in your room for a few days. You can come to the funeral if you want to, but stay away from the Farnsworths, especially Edward. After all this has had a few days to settle, I'll talk to the family and see what was going on. You didn't chase her up on that roof, but she didn't run to the edge until you went up there, so don't plan to leave Blessings for a while."

He hadn't wanted to leave Blessings at all, not without Lenora, anyway. Blessings had not proved to be the easy wealth he'd hoped for, and his mother was still waiting for him to come home. If only he could know what was happening back in England, if he was even wanted. Perhaps his family had just moved on without him. How many years did he have to try before he just admitted defeat, that he wasn't coming with the expected recompense, that he wasn't coming home because he couldn't face them after what he'd done?

"I'll sit in my little hovel for a few days, Sheriff. But I did nothing. I swear it."

Pete nodded and stood, his hands planted just above the twin Colts at his waist. "I don't believe you did, either. But beliefs and proof are two different things."

CHAPTER 15

Cort slid around the door to the little security office and moseyed over to the chair Pete had vacated about an hour before. Victor had yet to move. His life had taken a turn, and no matter how he tried to come up with a way out of the mess, he couldn't. Cort was welcome, because when Victor couldn't think of something, Cort had always filled in. When he'd been standing at the bottom of that ladder, waiting for Pete to go check on the other side of the house, he'd been sure that he was making the right choice, but now he wasn't so sure.

Cort slapped a deck of cards on the desk between them and leaned over as he shuffled it, staring at Victor. He could probably shuffle a deck in his sleep. He had an intense look about him that meant he had a lot on his mind. All the better to get answers.

"You and I both know that you weren't over messing around in Farnsworth's house. You were helping me build the livery for the past four days, we've got at least twenty men who will vouch for you. You haven't been out of my sight long enough to do anything."

That was true, but Mrs. Farnsworth was now gone. *She* wasn't going to tell them which days she'd been talking about in her cryptic declaration that he'd been after her in her house.

"Mr. Farnsworth is just angry, and sore. I would be too if my wife had just died. You can't take it personal or it makes you look guilty."

The cards flapped loudly against the desk and, for once, the sound irritated him.

"And have you gone to find *Miss* Farnsworth and made sure that she isn't *sore*?" Cort tilted his head and glared.

That was one thing he'd been hopping mad about. In fact, he'd taken the opportunity, in the empty room after the sheriff had left, to voice his opinion of being told to stay away from her. He hadn't even taken it seriously when her father had said it. Who was the sheriff to ask so much of him?

"I haven't yet, I'd planned to once I was sure she was done at Pati's."

"Our paint delivery should be in tomorrow. Are you going to be there to help me, or do I need to find a couple miners to do the job?"

Victor wanted to. The livery had been his idea and now that it was built, it was more and more something he could look on with pride.

"I'll be there. When is Mosier due to come in?"

Cort slapped the deck on the desk so Victor could cut it, then dealt five cards to each of them.

"Winslet says he usually gets here round about midday. So, we should gather ladders and anything else we'll need in the morning."

Cort's face was blank, as always. He was an excellent player, he'd yet to find Cort's tell. Victor looked at his own hand and, like his life at the moment, it was full of nothing. He laid down two cards and waited for Cort to hand him replacements. Still nothing. Everything in him told him to follow the path he always had, fold and run when he couldn't get what he wanted. Just like he'd done to his family.

"I'll be ready. I was just cooling down in here. The sheriff gave me orders and you know how well I listen."

Cort cackled as he laid down one card and drew one off the deck. They had no money to bet and he and Cort never wagered against each other anyway. But that didn't matter; his heart wasn't in the game anymore.

"You listen about as well as a rock, which begs the question, why are you still here? Miss Lenora left the company of the sheriff's wife a half hour ago, searched around a bit, then went home. I asked her if she was looking for you, but she wouldn't answer me. Wouldn't speak at all."

His heart clenched painfully in his chest. Would she look for him, or had he destroyed everything by ignoring the sheriff and climbing that ladder? Only Lenora could answer that question. Though the bravado he'd always felt told him to ignore the sheriff, his heart couldn't forget what had happened the last time. Maybe the sheriff knew more than he gave him credit for. Would both women be alive if he'd left well-enough alone?

"She is a stubborn one. If she was looking for me, I wouldn't still be waiting for her."

Cort laid down his hand in a practiced arc, a full house. "And *are* you still waiting for her?"

He glanced down at his own hand. Nothing, not even a pair.

"I will for as long as it takes."

"If that's true, then listen to the sheriff, as much as it will chafe you raw. Wait until she comes to you."

How he didn't want to hear that. He wanted to run to her even that instant.

"She might need me. She lost her mother

today." Dare he hope that she would accept his comfort?

"She's being fed a lie that it had to do with you. She'll need to work that over in her head, convince herself that you wouldn't do what you're being accused of. Remember, she was up on that roof, too. She knows in her head what you did, and didn't, do."

Victor understood as much, but his heart wanted to defend himself. "Wouldn't you want to defend your name?"

Cort swiped up all the cards and gave him a look fit to kill him. "If I'd ever been given the chance to prove why I'd done what I done, then I would have. I know it wasn't right to take that horse, but it wasn't right to steal what was mine, either."

Living under a lie was Cort's whole life. He would never be free of it, unless he was caught. Even then, he'd have to pray that he got a fair trial, and Cort wasn't a praying man.

"I hope that you get the chance to clear your name someday, friend. Unfortunately, I can't make that happen for you right now. Murder is a little more serious than horse thievery."

Cort hung his head. "I shouldn't have done it. When I heard that Freedman Gale, Coleman's son-in-law, was killed while chasing me...well, that's been eating at me something fierce."

Cort couldn't leave, he couldn't go back. It

was a sure death sentence.

"You aren't thinking of going back, facing the charges, are you? Going back won't bring that man back to life, won't bring back the horse. And it sure won't make Coleman sorry he stole those winnings from you."

"It was just money, Victor. I wanted the winnings so bad, I didn't even think about what it might cost him. Now that I'm here, and I've stopped running and searching behind every tree, I've had time to think about it. If I ever can get a plot of my own, or can make enough, I may try to make it right. He lost that hand fair and square, but that doesn't mean I had the right to take his horse."

If Cort could go back and make his past right, could Victor do the same? Could he go home and make all his poor choices right? Maybe he'd feel like a man good enough for Lenora if he did. His parents may never let him leave again, and living without Lenora wasn't a life worth living.

"We are quite the pair, aren't we, Cort? Two men who've made some wrong turns in our lives. I'm ready to give up. I just can't see the right path anymore."

"I'm not. Life's not worth living if it's not worth dying for."

Cort tapped the deck on the desk and stood. "You coming, or are you going to stay here until it gets too dark to see? Just because you can't go visit your gal, don't mean you don't have things to do. Let the sheriff sort out all the Farnsworth mess. Let me handle the rest."

The seamstress shack was the only bit of quiet Lenora could look forward to after two days with very little time to herself. She hadn't even allowed herself to mourn the loss of her mother, though they buried her almost right away. Late spring to almost summer in California was too hot to just leave her be. It had been an emotionless service for a town still in shock, but they hadn't known her. Most had never even seen her.

Oddly, as she'd helped prepare her mother for burial, she'd felt free, which then left her guilty. Her mother no longer feared the Indian attacks that hadn't happened, she didn't have to fight with anyone over who she was any longer... But she was also gone. There was no hope of happiness or redemption from her fears. Their last conversation played over in her head for long hours. Her mother had been so unhappy, trying to be who she wasn't. She'd let everyone tell her that who she was, right down to her skin, was wrong. The longer Lenora thought about it, the more it bothered her.

Though Victor had helped her off the roof, he hadn't found her after Pati had swept her away. He'd thoroughly disappeared, which wasn't like him. She'd needed to see him, to feel his strength. But he hadn't come for her. Now, days later, his new kerchief sat on the table of finished items, yet to be picked up. Pati had said they were not to deliver anything, but this wasn't just anyone, it was Victor, and she missed him. Pati might understand her need, she was newly married. But an order was an order and Lenora was too drained to ask.

Pati hadn't made her do the laundry, instead, offering her the chance to talk while helping her with her own embroidery. Pati told her of life in Ireland and in London, how she'd followed her father all the way to California, then stayed here when she met Pete. Pati seemed to understand that she didn't feel like talking, but listening was soothing. So, Lenora listened to Pati's stories from morning until late afternoon, when Pati was ready to go home. When Pati relaxed, and got into her story, her voice melted into an accent like a melody that soothed the rough edges of Lenora's thoughts.

Lenora's father had said he wanted her to work with him, but she had yet to stay in the office. He was angry, silent, brooding. She'd never seen him like that before. When he'd asked what had transpired up on the roof, she tried to explain, but her father seemed to have forgotten her mother's oddities since arriving in Blessings, and would only believe that somehow, the fault lay solely on Victor. Though in her heart she knew it was part of his grief, she couldn't abide him besmirching Victor. Not when he'd been the only one to value her life enough to climb the ladder and try to save them. She couldn't stand his accusations and hadn't allowed him to continue, but it didn't stop him from insulting Victor and talking to the sheriff about it.

Her father was furious that Victor hadn't been locked up. He wouldn't listen to reason and she hated going home in the evening. Even now, she let her gaze fall on the little square of fabric she'd worked so hard to finish, and only wanted to go to Victor, not her father. She hadn't even told Pati that her father wanted her to come back to work for him.

The livery was well out of her way, but that didn't stop her from glancing through the sparse trees, between the small houses and tents, all the way over where she could just see the roof of the stables. Mr. Mosier had arrived late the night before and she'd heard from one of the miners that Victor and Cort were painting. The building would soon be a nice bright red with white trim. No mail had come for her, but her father had received something from Boston. That was all she could see from the envelope, he hadn't shared anything further with her.

As she slipped inside the land office, her father sat at his desk with his head in his hands. His shoulders were slumped. He'd never allowed his emotions to show in his work, but now he couldn't seem to get a good handle on them.

"Father? Do you need something?" she spoke softly to keep from startling him. He hadn't raised his head when she'd come in.

"No, dear. The sheriff just stopped by and pointed out that Victor was with Mr. Nelson almost exclusively for an entire week, while they built the livery. When he wasn't with Cort, he was with you. I would guess that you would swear he never went up those stairs?"

Her heart raced. If Father would forgive him, perhaps she could risk going to Victor? But what then? He'd never let Father's rules stop him before, but he'd let *this*. The pain left a hole in her chest. His absence was all the more painful with her father's chilly demeanor.

"I would swear it. He never went near the stairs. I don't know what Mother saw, or whom, but it wasn't Victor. He's innocent."

Her father snorted his disagreement, but didn't speak further on it.

"Mrs. Winslet was kind enough to bring us our supper. It's upstairs on the back of the stove. I have no appetite. Eat if you'd like."

He stood and shrugged out of his business coat, draped it over his chair, and left her. She was free to go to Victor, but shouldn't he come to her? Wasn't she the one grieving? He'd said he would come check her progress on the kerchief every day, then he'd left her to herself. She pulled out the soft bit of embroidery she'd worked on that day, under Pati's watchful eye. It was just like the ones she'd made for Victor, with the same color pattern. The difference, this one had the initials LRA intricately embroidered in one corner. *Lenora Rose Abernathy.*

He'd already asked her, and she wanted to be with him, but her father had to agree, and Victor had to come for her. Her father would never wed them if he didn't. Soon, she would have to return to working with her father, and then all hope of Victor coming for her would be lost. She'd be expected to return to her father, and she would miss Pati, but now it was like a ticking clock in her head.

She couldn't bear to be in the house alone anymore. Even downstairs, where her mother had never been, still held her scent, her voice. If Lenora had believed in spirits, she would've fully believed her mother was still there. But she knew it was just her mind, wishing for what it could not have. Lenora ran up the stairs, refusing to even look at the window where she'd climbed out to follow her mother, and pulled the pan off the stove. She and her father would eat when they got hungry. But for now, like her father, she had to get out.

CHAPTER 16

Mr. Mosier arrived the following evening with a wagon load of supplies and the mail. The paint they had been waiting for had finally arrived. A few more days' work and they could open the livery. Mr. Mosier handed the mail bag to Mr. Winslet then started to unload the huge covered buckets of paint.

Victor didn't care much about the mail, but that paint wouldn't carry itself all the way across the settlement, back to where it needed to be. They were heavy, and there were four large buckets to move.

Atherton Winslet called his name with a rough laugh that had him more than a little surprised. The only one who knew he was in

Blessings was his mother, and he hadn't heard from her in years. His heart sank in his chest and felt heavier than pewter. If his mother was writing to him, she would be asking him to come home. Atherton handed him the letter, but didn't let go.

"Victor. You've got a look about you, and this letter didn't help none. Most people get good and happy when they get a bit of mail."

Victor tucked the letter into his vest pocket, so he could forget about it for a while. "It's nothing, sir. I'd just hoped to have a little more time, is all."

"Time? I've got more time than just about anythin' else. I'll give you some of mine. Use it wisely and tell me what's on your mind. You can't do anythin' with that paint this late in the day, anyway."

Atherton led them away from everyone vying for letters, over to a pair of stumps. Atherton sat first, then invited Victor to sit along with him. The paint would wait.

He hadn't had much time to talk to the founder of the town, though the old man made his way through the growing town many times a day, his wizened eyes and scrappy beard a familiar sight in Blessings.

Victor hadn't seen Lenora in over a day and he chaffed to rush over to the land office and ask for a walk, just so he could find out if she was getting on all right. He'd said he'd keep track of her progress on his kerchief, but then, the accident and the sheriff's warning had forced him to think. But it was Cort's suggestion that held him back. She would come to him when she'd decided he wasn't guilty.

"I've had my eye on a woman for over nine months. I've asked for her hand, but she hasn't answered. Her father isn't keen on the idea. I'd hoped to have more time to convince her that..."

He couldn't finish. In England, he'd been everything, had everything, he'd ever wanted. He'd considered himself the most important thing in every instance. Now, he saw it for what it was: a youth wasted.

"There a reason this woman hasn't given you an answer?" Atherton crossed his ankle over his knee, making himself at home on the stump.

"I've tried everything I know to get through to this woman, but it's no use. Not now. I had hoped this letter would never come. Now, I have to go home, and she's already said she will not go with me. I know that I need to go, that it's the right thing. My family is depending on me, waiting for me. Lenora isn't. She's got her father to care for her now. She'll find someone good enough for her."

The old man petted his mane of a beard for a moment. "Victor. Just 'cuz I didn't approve a job at the mine for you, doesn't mean you ain't a worthy man. I'd heard about your need to go back to England and, you see, now you must. The livery was a good investment, and it will still be there if you return. And if you love Lenora, you will."

Victor sighed and patted the heavy letter in his vest pocket. "I'm sorry, Mr. Winslet, I can't wait a moment longer."

He laughed but did not leave. "Go 'head."

Victor pulled the letter out and opened it, he could almost imagine the smell of his mother's lilac perfume, which she usually sprinkled over her letters.

Dearest Victor,

I hope I have waited long enough to write that this letter reaches you in California. I received your letter from last fall, saying that you would be moving all the way across America. I was quite surprised to hear that, since you would be moving even further away from us. The prospects for America must be far worse than I thought. I now regret suggesting you find your own fortune in the States.

I have some wonderful news. Your brother, Devin, made an excellent business decision and has now joined a man in a partnership that is sure to more than make the family fortune back, as long as we are patient. He has also married the most wonderful young woman, Adelle. She is simply lovely. I cannot wait for you to meet her. Devin tells me that you may meet her as long as you stay far away from her.

Your father has said that he misses you and wishes to speak to you. I hope you will take that as his forgiveness and come home. We all miss you. Your brother has said that if you come back, you will not be allowed to gamble away his money, so, if you return, bear in mind that you will have to work. Nathan and Ethan married sisters last spring. They shared a ceremony, and it was lovely. I wish you could have been there.

I miss you very much. It has been far too long, and it would do your dear mum proud if you would come home with expediency. The voyage is so long and arduous. I know you have probably just arrived in California and most likely have no desire to board a ship again so quickly, but if you make haste, perhaps you can even be back to us before the New Year. Wouldn't that be splendid?

Please let us know when you will be arriving. I will be watching for you.

Mum

"They don't need the money..." His mind

reeled with all the information. "All my brothers are married..." He was the only Abernathy yet alone. "Father wants to speak to me..." Which meant he was forgiven. After his last night of debauchery in England, his father had said he'd never speak to him again. Victor now regretted that night, as well.

"What's that?" Atherton cupped his ear as if he were hard of hearing. Victor knew better. He'd heard every word.

"My mother no longer needs the money. I don't have to go back... She misses me ... but I would miss Lenora too much. I don't have to go..."

He still couldn't believe it. The weight was off his shoulders. He wanted to run right over and tell Lenora, then kiss her until she answered him. Except, he'd agreed to stay away from her.

Atherton cocked his head to the side and glanced behind them, toward the river, a thoughtful relaxation taking over his face. Then he stared for a moment at the land office as if he was working out a problem in his head.

"I know you'll be busy the next few days or so, what with paintin' that stable and findin' a way to get a message to your family. I think, after that, you'll be done and ready for a break. I've got a little somethin' I need done down by the river, directly behind Pati's place. Can you meet me there, 'round three, in three days?"

What could Atherton need of him, unless the letter was proof enough that he wasn't going to leave, and Atherton was finally going to give him a job at the mine. His heart raced. Now that he didn't have to go, he could consider life in Blessings. If he could have that job, maybe that would be enough to convince Lenora's father to trust him, and then he could ask her once again. If he was good enough for Atherton Winslet, it might convince Lenora that he was a changed man. Oh, how he wanted to see her.

"Yes, sir. A day to paint and two days to travel to the nearest telegraph office. That'd be in Culloma ... there and back. I'll meet you by the river. Do I need to bring anything with me?"

The old man smiled with a twinkle in his eye as he stood from his stump and stretched.

"I'd say you should bring a smile and an open hand." He winked and walked away.

The slight breeze off the river was cool on Lenora's overheated face and the town sat quiet as most were inside, eating their noon meal. Though she'd never encountered Victor by the river, she couldn't help but hope that he would find her there, out in the open. What could possibly be keeping him away? Three days felt like a lifetime after being with him every day for almost a year.

To her right, she could hear the flume from the mine running water back to the river. To the left and behind, the town of Blessings nestled quietly in the little clearing. Everyone in town had been so resilient, moving on with life and encouraging her to do the same. Death was just another part of life, and though Blessings was more reserved than other places they had traveled through on their way, it was still a boomtown and fraught with danger.

Seraphina came from behind and sat beside her quietly, her cape in place, leaving her face buried in shadow, the sun never touching her skin. Her head was bent, almost like she was in prayer.

"I heard about your mother from my brother. I am so sorry," she whispered in her lilting French.

Lenora wished she knew more about the woman who kept herself so separate from the rest of the townsfolk. But today wasn't the day to learn her secrets.

"Thank you."

The woman reached within the depths of her cape and handed her a glass vial with a light green liquid. Even her hands were gloved.

"If you're having trouble sleeping. It will help. It's very strong. Put it in a cup, and top it off with water. Drink it like tea. It will help."

Lenora accepted it, but wondered if it was safe to take. She'd had no trouble with the salve for her hands, since that went on her skin, but wouldn't a witch make poison? Would it be safe? Seraphina had never done anything to hurt her, but the people of Blessings, people she loved and who had helped her through her trials thus far, were frightened of the quiet woman, save Pati. The salve Pati had given her gave her hope the whole town was wrong about Seraphina.

Seraphina ducked deeper into her hood as if terrified of the light.

"I should get back to my tent. I only venture out to get my herbs and water while everyone is working and won't notice me. My brother feels that it's best that way."

And with that, she stood and disappeared back from where she came. A few leaves rustling across the river caught her eye and she remembered the man she'd seen. Pati had assured her that, while seeing someone hiding was always unnerving, she respected the Miwok. They stayed on their side of the river and, as long as the people of Blessings did the same, there wouldn't be any trouble. They could both live in peace. But had one of the Miwok managed to come into Blessings? Had her mother been *genuinely* frightened? It seemed unlikely. It would be difficult for them to get around unnoticed.

Her mother's mind had been scarred by fear, and Lenora refused to let that happen to herself. She would be strong, she would help make Blessings a place where families would want to come for generations ... where her own generations could live. But only if Victor decided to come around again, because she couldn't imagine sharing her life or her heart with another man.

"Are you enjoyin' a little quiet by the river, Miss Farnsworth?" Mr. Winslet stood beside her for a moment then dropped onto the grass next to her.

She startled slightly; he'd come so quietly, she hadn't heard him approach.

"Yes, my home doesn't seem peaceful anymore."

"I'm sure it don't. With just your father here, will you be stayin' on in Blessings, or will you go to live with your brother?"

She hadn't even considered leaving, though perhaps people might think she wouldn't want to stay, now that her mother was gone. The opposite was true. Her mother had wanted to go so badly it had made living in Blessings difficult. If Geoff had taken Mother with him, Lenora would've breathed a sigh of relief and gone on, trying to find her own way.

"I'm not so sure about my father, but I, for one, would like to stay. There are people here that I couldn't live without, and I have nowhere to go once they leave."

The old man raised a bushy eyebrow and chuckled slightly. "That so? Are you sayin' there's someone here in Blessings who's more important to you than your father?"

It might sound strange, but she had to admit, at least to her heart, it was true. Victor meant more to her, and for the rest of her life, he would. She'd reached an age where she loved her father, but she needed a husband, someone to share her whole life with, someone to cherish her.

"I would say so, yes," she whispered, waiting for the old man to censure her for such an admission.

"Does this person know that you've set them to such esteem?" The old man leaned forward, catching her with wise hazel eyes that seemed much older than his years.

"No, not yet. It doesn't really matter, either. Because as much as I want life to change, it won't. He never stays anywhere long, and soon he will feel the urge to move along, far away. Maybe even home. He likes his women, you see, and one would never be enough for him." Her cheeks burned just saying it, but Mr. Winslet made anyone around him so at home, there was no need for pretense.

A strange twinkle glinted in the old man's

eyes. "I'm sorry to hear that, truly I am. I hate to see two people miss out on a life together, 'specially when I could grow old watchin' happy people." He shifted to his knees and plucked a strange little plant from in front of him.

"I came down to the river to gather a few things for the wife for cookin'—you know what kind of a cook she is—but it doesn't look like they're quite ready yet. Do you think you could meet me here tomorrow, about three in the afternoon, to help me? I need to gather quite a lot and ... well ... my old eyes. I can't see well enough to get what we need by myself."

He smiled, but there was more to what he was asking. His face fairly glowed with his exuberant smile ... and a secret.

Mr. Winslet had been so kind to her father, and so generous after her family had arrived in Blessings. She couldn't possibly tell him no, especially not after the Winslets had provided supper for them for a few nights after her mother had passed, even if most of the food had gone untouched.

"Of course, I'll help you. Are you sure the plants will be ready in time? It would seem this is rather, small." She picked up the little sprout that didn't look much different from common grass to her eye. "Does it mature quickly?"

The man laughed and slapped his knee. "It does mature quickly, 'specially when you feed and water it every day. I've got to go tell the wife. See you here tomorrow. Yes, definitely tomorrow. Don't be late!" He moved along down the bank and back toward Winslet House faster than she'd thought he could go.

The old man was so strange sometimes, though always well-meaning. Pati certainly wouldn't miss her for an afternoon and her father didn't seem all that concerned about having her underfoot in his office.

She knew so very little about cooking, though, her father knew even less. If Victor ever did come around again to get her answer, they would surely have to live with her father, or risk leaving the man to starve. Though, after just three days' absence, she had to admit she'd follow him all the way to Europe if that's what Victor wanted. Blessings was a wonderful town, staying there and watching it grow would be even better than becoming a lawyer. Without Victor, both her old dreams and the little town lost some of their luster.

Lenora shoved her new embroidered kerchief back in her pocket and found the path from the seamstress shop back to the main street that would take her home. But instead of taking it, she went farther down the new path that was soon turning into a trodden road, to the livery. Cort stood outside, his sleeves rolled up, mixing the paint with a long paddle. He glanced up from his work for a moment.

"Good afternoon, Miss Farnsworth. Come to take a look at the new paint?"

It was a lovely shade of red and it did make the building gleam in the bright sunlight.

"It looks good, almost done. Is your partner about? I haven't seen him in a few days."

Cort wiped his brow with a muscled forearm. "Sorry, miss. He worked with me until about noon, then he left for Culloma. He had to send a telegram to his mother. He got a letter from her when the paint came in and he wanted to make sure she got a reply quickly."

Cold dread washed down her spine. His mother had written to call him home. He might even be trying to book passage while he was there, if it was possible. And he would go alone, since she'd denied him what he'd been asking for. She prayed that he would have to go all the way to the coast for that. If he did, he'd have to come back to Blessings first. Then she could tell him her heart and go with him, if he still wanted her.

"How long do you think he'll be gone?"

"He had to walk, there was no horse or mule available. Could take him a little over a day. I'm sure he'll be back by tomorrow afternoon."

Why hadn't he come to see her, tell her he was going away? What if something happened to him and she never saw him again? He had to have left when she'd been down by the river. He could've been looking for her and hadn't found her.

"Is the road safe, you aren't concerned?" Not that it would help the painful burning within her. Even if Cort didn't fear for Victor, she would.

Cort laughed. "I taught him how to use the iron by his wallet. He may not be as good as me, but he's good enough that, unless someone comes upon him unawares, he'll be fine."

His reassurance did little to stop her empty stomach from swirling.

Cort stopped mixing the paint. "I'll let him know that you stopped by. He's been hoping you would. I told him to hold off, let you decide you were sure that he had no part in what happened."

And Victor had listened to Cort, that was why she hadn't had his presence when she'd wanted it? Didn't he see her as more important than Cort? Cort's words left an emptiness deeper than she'd expected. She'd needed to see if he could comfort her even better than he thrilled her, and Cort had kept her from knowing.

"His innocence was never in question, at least not with me. Victor had more important things to do than frighten my mother. My father insisted that we keep my mother's tender sensibilities under the table so that no one would think of her what they think about the witch. Superstition is rife where your livelihood is based on luck."

A deep laugh rumbled from Cort's chest. "That is true. I'm glad to hear that you know Victor's heart enough to know that he wouldn't do such a thing."

"It won't matter what I know, once he's gone." She left before he could respond. If Victor was leaving, at least his friend could give him the message that she, for one, wouldn't be happy about it.

CHAPTER 17

His calves burned from all the walking, but not more than his stomach. Victor hadn't brought much of anything with him, but the letter from his mum had distracted him from getting as much done on the painting as he should have. By lunch, Cort told him it would be good to go and get a note off to his mother and tell her just what she needed to know. He wasn't coming home. At least, not for a good long time.

Lenora was his life. He ached to see her after just three days apart. He thought he'd given up on prayer, but the last few days had found him praying for her. If he couldn't see her, couldn't hold her and comfort her, then he'd rely on the Lord to do it. His father would tell him he should've tried it sooner.

He'd gone to the seamstress shack just before he'd left, hoping to see her and tell her he'd be gone, but she hadn't been there. Pati couldn't or wouldn't tell him where Lenora had gone, and he'd had to rush or risk not making it back in time for his meeting with Winslet. That meeting could be the change his life needed. He'd quickly retrieved his new kerchief and left for Culloma.

After nine hours of walking he finally made it. He'd get right back on the road after his business in the morning and hopefully make it back in time. His belly and his feet had needs he couldn't presently ignore. Sending that letter would be declaring his independence, even more permanently than running away had. He wouldn't be living to run from his past anymore. His life would be his own once again, to live just as he pleased, and he would be pleased very much once Lenora was his.

Culloma was the town where gold had first been discovered in California, and it was a rowdy place. If he hadn't worn himself out of gambling since meeting Lenora, he'd have no trouble finding a table or two. And if not for Lenora, he would have even *less* trouble finding a few friends. The women waiting by the open windows of the saloons held little appeal. They didn't have a cloud of dark curly hair about their faces, the perfect rose lips. Nor were they modest enough to keep a man wondering about their beauty hidden from all eyes, because they hid nothing. Lenora would be his alone, *if* she believed in his innocence.

After reading his mother's letter, he'd stayed up most of the night, wondering about what he would say. Then it had been on his mind all the following day while he'd tried to help Cort. He was choosing to stay for Lenora, but she could easily never look him in the eye again. He hadn't even touched her mother, but his appearance had driven her off the roof and Lenora could blame him for that. The sheriff hadn't locked him up, but after telling him not to go up on the ladder, and the outcome of that poorly thought out decision, he certainly could've. When Victor wasn't praying for Lenora and for her heart to be soft toward him, he was reliving that moment on the roof over and over. She'd clung to him. And if *he* couldn't stop hearing the sound of Mrs. Farnsworth's demise in his own mind, how much more horrible for his poor Lenora? When he returned to Blessings, he wouldn't wait. He'd find her right away and make sure she knew his heart.

As he strode by the swinging front door of another saloon, he heard a familiar voice. Victor ducked inside and found Geoff sitting at a table in the corner. Victor slid into an empty seat as a man shuffled the cards.

"You looking to play, Abernathy?" Geoff snarled.

He wasn't. Geoff probably didn't even know about his mother yet and, sadly, he wasn't sure Geoff would care.

"You need to go on home, your father needs you."

Geoff shook his head and focused on his stack of chips in front of him.

"My father doesn't need me. He had no reason to need extra security for the trip. When I tried to work for him, he did nothing but pester me about going back to Boston to study to be a lawyer just like him. As if I would want to make that trip all the way back now. I'll make my own way."

Victor didn't want to tell the man about his mother in front of everyone, but there was no way he could know, and Victor couldn't just let it be.

"We should talk about this outside."

The men around the table sent shifty glances to everyone else. Calling a man outside could be seen as an invitation to fight, either with fists or guns, dependent on the men.

"I'd gladly meet you outside, you sorry excuse for a man."

Victor stood and leaned over the table, yanking Geoff to his feet.

"You'd best grow up a little bit before you go around insulting me. Turn in your chips and meet me outside."

His jaw was clenched so tight he'd crack his teeth if he didn't stop. If Geoff hadn't been Lenora's brother, he'd have just kept walking. But if Lenora cared about the man, even a little, then he had to.

Victor waited by the door as Geoff turned in his winnings and met him. He glared as he shoved out the swinging doors. How he wanted to put the insufferable boy in his place. While by most standards he was a man, Geoff had much to learn about being one.

He caught the door on its inward swing and followed Geoff out onto the street. People bustled all around them and Geoff took a gunslinger stance.

Victor took a deep breath. "I'm not here to fight you, Geoff. You're needed at home. Your mother took a turn and she didn't make it. Your father isn't taking it well. Your sister isn't taking it well, they need you. You want the chance to show them you're a man? Be one."

Geoff stared at him for a moment, then shook his head in disbelief.

"Are you trying to distract me? Did my sister tell you about Mother's sickness? Is she that close to you that she would air our business to you?" He spat the words.

He could hurt Geoff, make him wallow in his words, but it wouldn't help him, and it wouldn't make Geoff go home.

"What your mother did was in front of the whole town. Your sister did nothing but try to help a horrible situation, one that could have been helped by you offering to take your mother. You need to either go back to Blessings and become a man and be there for your father, or go far away. Your father doesn't need you to be a petulant child right now."

Geoff was barely eighteen, but he'd been spoiled in Boston. He hadn't been ready to take on the responsibility to watch his family on the ship and Mr. Farnsworth had known his wife would need him, so he'd hired Victor, and Victor would forever be thankful. Edward's agreement to include Cort would remain a mystery, but that didn't matter anymore.

"A petulant child? You mean like someone who tosses his father's money to the wind and then gets scolded and sent off to fix it?"

Geoff was hurting, and no one had bothered to try to understand him, but there came a point when he had to be a man. Sometimes hurts needed to be put aside and dealt with later. His family needed him to do just that, but he wasn't ready.

"Are you going back?"

Geoff turned and glanced over his shoulder.

"No. I see no reason to ever set foot in Blessings again."

It would hurt Mr. Farnsworth even more to know that he'd seen Geoff, told him of his mother's death, and he'd still walked away. He'd learned after so many months with Lenora that honesty was the best way to keep your head on straight. She'd taught him that. He wouldn't live a life of dishonesty and debauchery any more. Though, if Geoff remained on his current path, he would have to wade through that himself.

Now, even his head was bone-weary. He found the nearest boarding house that didn't look like it might blow over in a stiff wind and paid eight times what it would've cost for a room anywhere else in the whole of America. The walls were thin, and he missed his quiet bed in Blessings. Talk and all sorts of other noise came from the other sides of the calico hung up as walls between each room. One poor woman a few beds over cleared her throat all night long whenever she heard the intimate night noises so easily heard through the thin fabric walls.

When he could no longer pretend to try to sleep, he left his pallet and paid for his room and a breakfast at over a dollar a plate. He'd have to leave town soon or completely clean out his pockets. Culloma had a small post office and he took the short sheet of paper for a telegraph to the counter to write it out. Every word would be expensive, and he had to make each one count.

MUM, LETTER COMING. GOOD TO HEAR
FROM YOU. I'M STAYING IN CALIFORNIA.
- VICTOR

The short missive seemed cold when he read through it again, but he would write a full letter and send that along while he was here as well, but a full letter would take over a month to arrive. While he wasn't sure how quickly she would get the telegraph, it would be quicker than a letter, and he didn't want her to worry.

He composed a message, telling his mother about Cort, Blessings, and the woman who had captivated more than just his body. His mother had warned him all those years ago that there was a woman somewhere who would be his match in every way, and she would turn his wandering head to the straight and narrow. Mum couldn't have been more right.

Though his legs still ached from the long walk the day before, he wasn't going to be gone from Blessings for more than a day if he could help it, and he was for sure not going to stay another night in an expensive calico box. Blessings called, but it's voice was Lenora's.

The worry ate away at Lenora. Every few

minutes, she searched out her window to the east, hoping to see Victor return. Though Cort had said he wouldn't be back yet that day, she had hoped. Three days without seeing Victor would now turn into four. She'd lain awake, listening to the rustle of the trees outside, and praying that he'd made it safely to Culloma. If he'd had to spend the night, he wouldn't be home for hours. She let the heaviness of her thoughts weigh her down.

Pati would be waiting for her, no matter how tired she was after her sleepless night. Lenora would need to warn her boss that she would need to leave early that day, at about three when Mr. Winslet would need her help. Pati was so sweet, she would probably offer to come along and help.

She got dressed and left her room to find that her father had already gone down to his office for the day. The whole town had done their best to leave him alone after Mother died, but the growing town still needed him. Slowly, he would return to his busy usual. At least he had his friendship with Atherton to get him through. Lenora managed to eat a little of the leftover supper from the night before. She and her father weren't hungry, so each meal served to feed them longer, which made sure that she didn't have to cook.

As she came down the stairs, her father sat

at his desk, writing.

"Lenora," he said quietly. It was the closest he ever came to wishing her a good day anymore. Her heart ached for the strong man who had been taken down so thoroughly. He'd never been an affectionate man, but he'd loved her mother.

"Is there anything I can do for you, before I go off for the day to help Pati?"

He lifted the papers and tapped them against his desk. "No, I should think I would be fine here. There hasn't been much work of late. Perhaps when I get busy again, you can return here as we spoke about before your mother's accident."

He was so quiet, not the man who had made the decision to come all the way to California and strike out on a new path, far from Boston.

"Have you lost your way, Father?" the words slipped out before she could fully think them through. Of course, he had. Mother had been part of him for so long.

He sighed heavily. "I'm afraid I have. I was so angry with your mother for distancing herself, for trying to change my mind about coming here. She hated Boston and all the lies, so I thought she would be happy here, in this quiet little pocket of California. She wouldn't have to tell anyone her past if she didn't want to, she could just live. But all those rules she claimed to hate so much were a constant for her, comfortable. She knew just how to act and what to say. She couldn't do that here. All the way to Blessings, as she mourned the loss of her home while on the ship, she convinced herself Blessings would be a horrible place. Then Mr. Abernathy suggested there were Indians just waiting in the shadows to take any unsuspecting woman hostage, and from that point forward, she wouldn't be dissuaded that they weren't everywhere, just hoping for her to have a minute alone."

She swallowed hard. Lenora hadn't made the trip any easier on her mother. "I thought her fear started once we got here."

He shook his head. He'd seemed to turn grayer by the day.

"Remember when we got here, I told you not to judge Abernathy based on rumors? I did. I knew he wanted your heart with all that was in him and I let those rumors rule me. Geoff had no proof of what he claimed, but I believed. I shouldn't have trusted anything from your mother's mouth, especially not in the state she was in just before she died, yet I did. I'm sorry, Lenora. It must have been terribly difficult to live with me, hoping every day that the man I told you to trust, that I practically bade you to love, would be trusted by me. Can you forgive me?"

She'd been angry with her father, but would

never dream of holding it against him, and certainly not now.

"Of course, Father." She moved to the front of his desk and took his clammy hand. "We must stick together now. Without Geoff, all we have is each other."

He laughed humorlessly. "No, my dear. I believe that when Victor comes back from his little jaunt, he won't be able to wait a moment longer to see you. If he asks you, what will you say?"

Did she dare tell him that he'd already asked her? Would he be angry that Victor had not gone to him first?

"He *has* asked, in a roundabout way." She met his glance and he urged her to go on with an arch of his eyebrow. "I would say yes, if he asked again."

Her father smiled slightly. "Good. I don't want to have to worry about you, and you shouldn't have to worry about me, anymore. Don't make him ask you again. You have my blessing, Lenora."

She couldn't just leave him, not after losing Mother.

"What if he wants to take me to England, what then?"

He leaned softly against the desk, as if he were weak.

"We will deal with that when and if it

happens. Until then, you'd best get to Pati, she's probably wondering where you are."

For the first time in days, the road to the seamstress shack felt light. Father was beginning to heal and see the truth, and Victor would be home later that day, if Cort was right about the distance and the time it would take.

Pati waited for her outside the seamstress shack as usual, a slight smile on her face that grew larger as she looked up.

"Good morning! Mr. Winslet stopped by earlier to tell me that he needs you this afternoon. Very strange that he would pick you of all people to help him out, but he asked that I let you go a little early, so I will."

"Thank you." Lenora could think of nothing else to say about it. She knew nothing of plants and Mr. Winslet's choice baffled her most of all.

"Mr. Abernathy's kerchief is gone..." Lenora hadn't noticed before she'd left for lunch the day before, and she hadn't returned to work after, but it was no longer on the table with the finished items.

"Yes, while you were at lunch yesterday he came in. I forgot to tell you. Also, he wanted to order one more, but this one is different. Though, the work is already done." She smiled again as she drew a small slip of paper from her pocket.

"He wants the same three colors as before

except he doesn't want the A black on this one, he wants it red."

Red? If the blue was for her eyes, and the rose for her lips...why red?

"Red? Did he say why?"

"No, but look at the design." She handed the paper to Lenora. The paper almost slipped from her fingers as she opened it. It was the design she'd already made for herself, with the initials *LRA*.

"Oh..." words failed on her tongue. He'd left her for days, but when he'd come to find her, she'd been gone. His message was clear. He still wanted her for his bride, and he *would* come back for her. Her heart beat so quickly she couldn't contain her joy, she wanted to run to find him, but she didn't know the way. She clutched the paper in her trembling fingers.

"I'll get started on it right away. He could be here for it later today."

Pati got herself situated with a dress on her stool. "Yes, he may. I should've told you yesterday, but you didn't return after luncheon."

"I love him, Pati." She had to tell someone, or she would just burst. She'd held her feelings in check for so many months because he wasn't the *right* man, and because he was going to leave, but it didn't matter anymore. Someone had to know.

"I know. I've known from the first time I saw

you two together. That isn't something you can hide."

"So, you think he knows it, too?" She prayed he did, that he'd seen through her attempts to control herself; that he could see her heart.

"I think he has a good idea of how you feel, but you should probably tell him. Men aren't as good at reading that kind of thing as women. They can be as slow as a spring drizzle. A good strong woman doesn't need a man to say first what needs to be said."

Pati always was good for speaking plainly.

"You're right, and I'd better get to work. I don't think I could get it done before he gets here."

She laughed and handed her a seam ripper. "Tear out the A on the one you've already got and just change the color. You can make a matching one for yourself later."

And she would, she would also make matching pillow cases and a quilt for their bed, assuming he would give her that much time. Mr. Abernathy didn't like to wait, and she'd already put him off for months. Once he learned that he was back in her father's good graces, she may not be able to make him wait a moment longer. Not that she wanted to.

CHAPTER 18

The farther the sun got past its zenith, the faster Victor tried to walk. He'd have to pick up his pace to make it on time. He'd really hoped to go and see Lenora first, even bring her to the river to meet with Mr. Winslet with him. If she could see for herself that he'd changed enough for Atherton to grant him a job, she would accept him. He felt it right down to his toes.

As he made it into Blessings, the silence around Winslet House met him. He'd have to go right to the river. Atherton wasn't sitting on his front stoop as he usually did to keep an eye on his town. Victor pressed on, even though his legs were so sore he could barely keep them straight.

He'd rest once his had his promise from Atherton, and his Lenora.

Dodging around trees, he made it to the river's edge and followed it farther east, down by the mines. As he came closer, Atherton wasn't there. He paused for a moment and stared. There, by the river, was the woman he'd wanted to see all along. Had Atherton known that this would change her mind? Could that be *why* he'd agreed to meet him, in order to give Lenora reason to trust him? He pressed forward and Lenora glanced up, her deep blue eyes wide. As soon as she recognized him, her face shifted from surprise to utter elation. A healthy pink infused her cheeks and her eyes brightened as she smiled. She took his breath away. A woman had never been so happy to see him.

She shifted to face him, and he had to hold himself in check. The desire to crush her close and kiss her until she knew just how much he'd missed her was so strong he could taste it.

"Victor." She glanced up into his eyes, tilting her chin just so. "I've missed you."

"Did you?" He held his breath for a moment. "Not half as much as I've missed you, love."

She flinched, and pain suffused her face for a moment and he couldn't stop himself from rushing forward, taking her hands in his. They were so soft, now that it had been days since she'd done wash for Pati.

"What is it, darling?" If he'd done something to hurt her, he had to make it right. Everything had to be perfect when Atherton came.

"How could you miss me? I haven't seen you for days and you've only been gone from Blessings for one."

He cupped her cheek and let his hand trace all the way to the soft tendrils of hair at her nape, then tugged her close, finally holding her as he'd wanted to.

"My lovely Lenora. I was told first by the sheriff to stay away, then Cort agreed with him. They were sure you might be hurt by my involvement in your mother's death. I never meant for that to happen, and I never went near her, Lenora. You have to believe me."

Her arms encircled his waist and held him tight. Many women had pressed themselves to him, but none fit so well, none were as welcome, and none as precious.

"Oh, Victor. I never thought for a moment that you did. I just needed you. I needed to know that you cared about me ... more than you have about every other woman in your life. When you didn't come around ... I was sure that I was just another skirt in a long line." Her voice hitched, and he held her tighter.

"Never. You were never like them. From the first moment I saw you, I had to know more about you, had to be near you. You are more precious to me than any woman anywhere. I can't fathom why you would give me your attention at all, but I'm blessed beyond measure that you do."

She pulled away slightly and tilted her head back to look him in the eye and, again, took his breath away. They were bright with unshed tears.

"What about your family and your promise to make money and return?"

"My mother sent me a letter. All three of my brothers are wed and doing well. They miss me, but they don't need me to come back. I'm free, Lenora. I know you could do so much better than a poor livery owner who's seen far too many saloons. But—"

She held a soft finger to his lips, stopping him.

"Victor. I love you. It matters not to me how you make your living. As long as you work hard to provide for me and our children, I will be a happy woman."

His heart raged against his chest, and he kissed her finger. When she laughed and cupped his cheek instead, he took his chance and captured her lips. She squealed in surprise, then melted into him as he lifted her off the ground. His legs quaked both with the power of her kiss and with the fatigue. He'd have to find somewhere to set her, but he wasn't ready to let her go. As he let her slide back to solid ground, she sighed, and parted from him much too soon.

"Will you stay with me forever, Victor? Or will you tire of me?" She bit her lip and her sweet eyes danced from his lips just before she wrapped her arms around him to hide under his chin.

"Love, I will never tire of you. You could kiss me like that every day until the Lord takes you home and I'd never be weary of it."

"Yes."

He laughed, suddenly unsure of himself, which was a whole new feeling for him.

"Yes? What are you agreeing to?"

"Yes, I'll marry you. As soon as you'll have me. But I have one request."

"Anything." He couldn't breathe. Sweet mercy, where would he and Lenora live, how would he ever make a home for her, and where was Atherton?

"My father will do a wedding for us whenever you want it, but when the circuit preacher comes back to town, I'd like to say our vows before God."

Praying had kept Lenora safe when he couldn't be near her, and had brought her to him when he was sure she'd want nothing to do with him. He couldn't deny her such a small request after he'd relied so heavily on a God he was sure hadn't wanted anything to do with him. But would the Lord agree that he should be anywhere near a church?

"I don't think God wants me in His house, love. You may be willing to overlook my past, but there aren't enough Hail Marys to wash away all I've done. I wouldn't even be able to recall it all."

"You can't, but He can, and you won't have to say a single Hail Mary, the preacher is Protestant." She giggled.

He kissed her head and held her close. "My mother will already cry that I'm not coming home, I won't tell her that I'll be absolved by the Protestants. That might be more than my poor mum can take."

She laughed again. "Does that mean you will?"

"Yes, love. I'll step foot in the church if it means I can see that smile again."

Lenora sighed once again. "I wonder where Atherton is?"

He couldn't help his surprise. "You were meeting Atherton? I'd thought perhaps he'd sent you here to meet us? I wasn't sure why else you would be here."

She shook her head. "No, I was supposed to meet him here to pick some plants."

"He asked me here to ... work. But I thought he was going to give me a job and my own plot to build on."

"I don't think so. He only does that through

Father, and he's had almost nothing to do since Mother's accident."

"So he..." Atherton had made sure they would both be in the private little glen by the river at the same moment, and both of them with the same needs. The wily old man had known. Victor would never be able to repay him.

"He what?" Lenora searched his eyes.

"Nothing, love. Let's go talk to your father."

EPILOGUE

Pati had wanted to make her a gown, but there just wasn't time to get fabric and do all the sewing. They had settled for taking one of her mother's gowns and adjusting it to fit Lenora. Just two short weeks after she'd agreed to be Mrs. Abernathy, she would walk down the aisle to her husband. Since her father was officiating, as the circuit preacher only came once every three months, Mr. Winslet would stand in as her father, and he seemed almost happier than she was about it. He fairly danced when she'd asked him to participate in the ceremony.

Now she stood at the front of the church as everyone in the little town sat waiting for the service to begin. Victor was very unsure in his faith, but he loved her more than she'd ever felt before, and they were moving forward. Victor may never be chosen to do a sermon on a Sunday, but he'd sat next to her the last two Sunday's and even managed to look interested. It was progress. He did believe, she just had to convince him the Lord could forgive him, and what better way to do it, than to show him love?

The women of Blessings started a hymn and Lenora moved to her spot at the end of the aisle. Victor waited for her, his eyes taking her in and appreciating every bit. Hopefully, he would remember this day just as much as she would. This was their compromise. They had their service in a church, but officiated by her father. Then they wouldn't have to do anything over again. She'd hoped for a true preacher, but her father was a man of God, and it would have to be good enough. All that mattered was that she would be with the man she loved, and she would say her vows in a church.

As she reached Victor, Atherton gave her a kiss on the cheek and slipped her hand into Victor's. Victor squeezed it as he slid her hand under his elbow and walked her the last few feet to the front. Her wonderful man had always seemed so very sure of himself. Today, he looked nervous. He'd already told her that he feared he would let her down, that he wouldn't be enough for her. She gripped his arm until he looked down at her, and she smiled. At the sight of her smile, his muscles relaxed under her fingers immediately, and the service went faster than she could imagine.

She turned to look at all the faces of the residents of Blessings. This was her new extended family, but Victor was her life, her heart, and her forever—and she was blessed beyond measure to be his wife.

Thank you, dear reader, for joining me on this adventure. I hope you've enjoyed it and that you'll continue reading the next book in the series, *Hell-Bent on Blessings*.

Be sure to join my special reader list to find out when the next Brides of Blessings novel will be released. You can also get a free book at www.KariTrumbo.com.

Other Books by Kari Trumbo:

Cutter's Creek Series:

Montana Trails
A Lily Blooms
A Penny Shines
A Carol Plays
A Ruby Glows
An Ivy Tangles
Keepsake

Western Vows Series

To Honor and Cherish
For Richer or Poorer
To Love and Comfort

Seven Brides of South Dakota

Dreams in Deadwood
Kisses in Keystone
Love in Lead
Romance in Rapid
Sparks in Spearfish
Hearts in Hot Springs
Seven Brides Boxed set

Contemporary series Whispers in Wyoming

Heartstruck and
Heavensent
Temptation and
Tenderness

EXCLUSIVE SNEAK PEEK AT
HELL-BENT ON BLESSINGS

Harriet heard the two men speaking in hushed tones on the boardwalk as she exited the mercantile. It didn't surprise her that Jackson Davis would whisper behind her back—the banker in town, it seemed he had very little to say to any woman. But why was Jason whispering? Sundown's sheriff, he was usually quite polite and conversational. She turned her head to look over her shoulder and almost stopped walking, but decided whatever they were discussing didn't matter. She had chores and the children would be home from school soon.

She strolled on, but a moment later, Jason called her name. She slowed and turned. "Good afternoon, Jason."

"Afternoon, Harriet."

He was a stunningly tall, good looking man. Warm, blue eyes that seemed to caress your skin and a gleaming white smile had every unmarried—well, and *married*—female in town at least daydreaming about him. Except for Harriet. Her beloved husband Henry had soured her on love, romance, and all the fairy tales associated with happily-ever-afters.

"Um," Jason tugged off his dusty Stetson,

revealing slightly sweaty, curly blond hair. "I was just wondering if you'd seen Henry in the last few days."

The mere fact that he asked if she'd seen her own husband recently spoke volumes about what folks knew of her married life. No secrets in a small town. "Not in a week or so."

"A week? Is that normal?"

She shrugged and tried to keep any shame from her expression. "Not unheard of." Jason rubbed his chin, glanced back at the mercantile. Jackson Davis ducked inside, as if he hadn't been watching. Harriet narrowed her eyes at Jason. "Something going on I need to know about?"

Jason fluttered his lips in apparent indecision, but after a moment, he shook his head. "No. Nothing." He pursed his lips like he wasn't happy with that answer. "Soon as he shows up, you'll tell him to find me or see Jackson?"

Harriet crossed her arms and drummed her fingers, debating how concerned she should be. It didn't seem likely Jason was going to give her any more information. She cast a glance at the mercantile. Davis definitely wouldn't discuss anything with her. Henry probably owed a debt somewhere. Long as they didn't try to collect from her; of course, that was a possibility. Her money, according to territorial law, was more

Henry's than hers—even though she'd certainly done more of the work around the ranch to earn it. "I should be worried, shouldn't I." It was not a question.

Jason heaved a deep sigh and his brow furrowed with an honest expression of grief. "I'm sorry, Harriet, I can't discuss it with you. You'll send Henry our way, soon as you see him?"

"Soon as I see him."

Made in the USA
Coppell, TX
07 September 2020

36915815R00142